FURY, SON OF THE WILDS

*The mare stood over him, trying to lick him clean
and to comfort him*
[p. 10]

FURY

SON OF THE WILDS

HAZEL M PEEL

GIETE

Copyright © H M Peel 1959
First published in 1959 by George C Harrap & Co Ltd
Reprinted 2011 by Giete
Loundshay Manor Cottage, Preston Bowyer
Milverton Somerset TA4 1QF
www.wallispeelbooks.com

Distributed by Gardners Books
1 Whittle Drive, Eastbourne, East Sussex, BN23 6QH
Tel: +44(0)1323 521555 | Fax: +44(0)1323 521666

British Library Cataloguing in Publication Data
A catalogue record for this book is available from the British Library

ISBN 978-0-9547268-8-1

Typeset by Amolibros, Milverton, Somerset
This book production has been managed by Amolibros
Printed and bound by T J International Ltd, Padstow, Cornwall, UK

TO ROY

There are men both bold and great,
Who hold that in a future state,
Dumb creatures we have cherished here below,
Will give us joyous greetings as we pass the
    golden gate,
Is it folly if I trust it may be so?

From the tomb of a horse in Dublin

Contents

Illustrations

CHAPTER ONE

The Foal

THE wild horses moved together uneasily as the tropical storm increased in violence. Heads lowered, quarters turned to the driving rain with tails firmly tucked down, they bunched together for comfort.

The lightning stabbed at the dark sky in jagged flashes, throwing eerie shadows from the stunted trees, momentarily lighting up the bunch of horses, and vanishing, to leave them in darkness blacker than before. The thunder clapped and echoed in their ears as they stood patiently waiting for the storm to end.

The rain slanted down in streams, to beat harshly upon any living thing bold enough to defy its force. And it was as the storm climbed to its frenzied peak that the brown mare decided to drop her foal. She had moved into a slight hollow which was sheltered by an old gum-tree, but even there the rain beat down fiercely on her recumbent form.

She heaved and strained convulsively, her flanks shaking. Her ears were wet with sweat as well as rain, and her breath came in huge sobs. Suddenly the foal slid out on to the wet earth. The mare rested a second, then struggled to a sitting position. She licked away the enveloping bag, then she sank back, exhausted.

The tiny foal lifted his large, grotesquely ugly head and struggled feebly. He had to do something, but he was not sure what. Down went his head again into the mud. Then the fierce drive of instinct told him to stand and live, not lie down and die. The same compelling force was working in the mare. Her foal must suckle, and therefore she must stand. Without the precious milk she knew her baby would die. She jerked her forelegs out, strained, and with a huge effort was erect again. The rain seemed to beat down even more fiercely, and for a second she wilted; but natural instinct prevailed, and she turned and nudged the foal.

The tiny creature sensed the urgency of the nudge and struggled up. With an effort he managed to stand, but the four long, spindly legs teetered uncertainly; the large head drooped, and the tiny squiff of a tail was tucked tightly down against the small quarters.

The mare swung herself into position and pushed the foal's head under her body. She waited, but the foal did not suck. Something was stirring faintly in his mind. He had to do something, he must do something, but what? The driving rain was battering his tiny body, threatening his life before it had properly begun. The mare swung round, butted the foal sharply, and then moved back again into position. The foal's head slipped on to the teat, and he started to suck.

The mare, gaunt and haggard, stood still, hunching her body as the rain squalled from a fresh direction. The foal pulled and sucked, little rivulets of milk coursing down from his small mouth. At last he was satisfied, and for the moment at peace. The mare stood over him, shielding him from the rain with the bulk of her own body, trying to lick him clean and to comfort him. His stomach full, the foal now became aware of another need, and his legs buckled as he sank to the ground to sleep. The mare swung herself round to take the full force of the wind. She lowered her head and half closed her eyes, keeping her ears back and her nostrils half-dilated as sentinels.

So the black colt foal was born into the vastness of the Australian outback, by a brumby stallion out of a thoroughbred mare. And he was to become known as Fury, the Son of the Wilds.

For years the brumbies, or wild horses, had roamed the spinifex plains, the gum-tree slopes, and the arid hills, unhindered by man or beast. Occasionally some wandering boundary rider would come across the herd—the mares and foals cropping the short grass, and the stallion standing on some near-by hill-top, where he could command not only a good view of his charges but also see the approach of any enemy.

The stallion was a huge animal, with an ugly scar on his left cheek-bone, a reminder of some long-past battle for the herd's supremacy. He very rarely had to battle hard now. Years of leadership had taught him whom to tolerate and whom to kill. The young colt foals he ignored with majestic grandeur. They were too far below him to warrant even a passing glance. The yearling colts sometimes attracted his notice, but any attempts at familiarity on their part were quickly dispelled by snapping teeth and flailing hooves. The rising two-year-olds he watched more carefully. They were often bold enough to challenge him for the leadership of the herd. But when they did the outcome was inevitable.

The stallion would descend from his lofty position to the attack. The confidence of his challengers always blinded them to the stallion's advantage of higher ground, and when they rushed to meet him, the stallion, taking his time and waiting for the correct moment, would launch his huge body against them from above, transformed by rage into a fighting fury.

Rearing, biting, wheeling, and kicking, he made his onslaught, and the result was always the same. A savage hoof descended, a weird scream of animal rage and triumph rent the air, and an inert form was left to the dingoes.

The foal's mother had not been a member of the brumby herd for long, and Fury was her first foal by the stallion. She was a rangy-looking mare, with fine-boned legs that hinted at great speed. She had once been a flat racer, but had always proved a doubtful and most erratic starter at the gate. At last, after spending and losing many pounds on entry fees, her owner had gladly sold her to a north Queensland station owner for riding.

She had proved herself a useless and unpredictable stock-horse too, and when one night she had broken out of her yard and galloped off into the bush, lured by the stallion's calls, her new owner had written her off as a bad business investment.

The tiny foal, full of his mother's milk, content, and shielded from the storm, slept peacefully, unaware of his mixed heritage —half wild, half thoroughbred.

When Fury awoke the rain had stopped, and there was a sweet, clean smell in the air which made him crinkle his nostrils in anticipation. He sensed with pleasure the freshness of the wet earth, the sharp, wholesome smell from the gum-tree, and the already familiar closeness of his mother.

His tiny head lifted, and he blinked uncertainly as the sun pointed yellow fingers across the sky. He felt a gentle warmth on his back, and although he did not look up at the sky, he felt that the sun was good and friendly, like his mother. He pushed out his forelegs, heaved, and suddenly he was standing upright, with only a faint wobble. The mare fussed around in pride, nickering encouragement, and he pushed his head forward and sucked again. Satisfied once more, he looked around. His eyes could not focus properly yet, and although he could see the other horses around him, distant objects were blurred, unknown, and frightening, and he leant against his mother in sudden fear.

Then he moved one dainty and perfectly formed hoof and executed his first step, then another and another. Then, exhausted by his first trial, he turned to the mare and demanded a reward. His tiny head pushed vigorously, and the milk started to trickle out of the corner of his mouth, down the baby fuzz on his face to the delicate whiskers. He swished his squiff of a tail in pleasure and tentatively tried a few more steps.

Everything was so fresh and exciting! He had nothing to fear, because alongside him was his mother, nickering and butting her head in encouragement.

During the next few days Fury found out how to control his ungainly legs in the trot and canter. He ventured to go a few paces from his dam, but always in a circle, keeping her in the middle. At first his ridiculous legs had threatened to trip him up, but gradually he mastered them, and his steps became firmer as his confidence increased.

After the storm the grass had quickly grown rich and thick, covering the bush-land in a glorious carpet of greenness, spreading right to the top of the hills, varying in depths of colour, blending and harmonizing with the shades of the trees. The crickets had stopped their fiddling for a time, and the frogs had taken over, with their deep, full-throated croaks starting hesitantly in the evening, rising to a crescendo as the moon rose, and keeping up a dull, pounding tone through the night.

The birds had found fresh energy during the day-time, and the vivid parakeets flitted across the trees in brilliant, swift flashes of rainbow colour. The kookaburras had once more started to jeer at the world with their insane laughter, and even the kangaroos and wallabies seemed full of fresh vigour.

Fury revelled in the feeling of the long, thick grass. His hooves jolted cockily on the turf, and he sometimes felt an urge to do something to his back, so springy and exhilarating was the grass.

As the weeks passed by he lost some of his babyishness and began to copy his dam. The first time that he had eaten grass had been an astonishing and wonderful moment. Watching his dam pulling the green stuff had intrigued him, and he had to copy, only to let the stuff drop from his mouth in puzzlement. But he soon learned the importance of snapping the fronds of grass with a clean movement, and delighted in rolling them lusciously around his mouth, as the taste became familiar. Slowly, as he discovered grass, so he forgot his mother's milk and began to acquire an enormous curiosity about what went on around him.

He had lost a little of the ugly looks of his birth, and his body had started to develop a more vertical line. He had complete control over his legs and he found a wild delight in galloping madly round his mother. Now he found another great delight in the company of other young foals like himself. His curiosity soon led him into trouble. He would boldly trot up to any mare and attempt to get a free feed, and more than once this led to a sharp outburst of animal temper between the mare concerned and his dam.

He became aware of the stallion very slowly. He had seen him standing aloof on one side, higher than the herd, but Fury's young mind was not yet interested in anything that was not close to him. He was intrigued by the way the mares followed the great horse and by the way the other colts respected him. To the stallion Fury was but another foal, small, young, and insignificant. He must be watched over and guarded, but as yet he was no danger to the stallion himself.

Now and again the stallion's great, magnificent head would lift from the grass, and he would watch the scene below him, his powerful eyes resting on the foals. For some reason unknown to him and not understood by him, he would watch the small black colt foal longest of all. It was as if he was seeing himself as a young animal—seeing a small black miniature of bounding energy pushing forward into life, exploring and adventuring into the unknown.

The first time that Fury clashed with the stallion was early one morning. He had started to wander a little to one side of his mother and the other foals. Somehow, it was not so very important now for him always to stay near his mother, and this morning the urge to wander was strong.

He saw a morsel of grass growing green and thick half-way up the slope where the stallion stood. He scrambled up the side of the hill and greedily began to gobble as fast as he could. Then, to his shock and horror, he felt a sudden pain in his right quarter. Fear and surprise gave him speed; he whipped round and found himself looking into the baleful eye of the stallion. The great mouth opened and the ugly teeth threatened again, and Fury turned and fled as fast as his legs could take him back to the safety of his mother, away from the frightening presence of his sire.

From then on he was more aware of the stallion. He was afraid of him, he knew that, but he did not know why he was afraid, and when his courage was strong he would gamely trot towards the slope and look long and hard at the figure on the hill. The powerful body, the large, well-formed muscles, the fire and spirit that shone from the baleful eyes stirred something inside the foal's body that puzzled him, and when he returned to the security of his mother he was uneasy and unsettled.

Fury no longer simply wandered in a circle about his dam now. He would gallop wildly away from her, then turn round and race back as quickly as he could, while she placidly continued pulling at the grass. He would slither to a halt, then turn round and race away again. So he rid himself of surplus energy and began to build up strength in his muscles.

The day came when he trotted independently away from his dam on a quest of adventure, and she did not call him back. He joined the other foals, and together they played a frenzied game of galloping over the bush.

On days when the grass was very springy he had an uncomfortable feeling in his back, but one morning he discovered how to cure it. He learnt how to buck, that all-important and exhilarating form of exercise peculiar to well-bred and high-spirited horses. Down would go his head, up would go his back, and for five minutes or more he would indulge in this pastime, leaping high into the air, coming down with hard, propping jolts, and then turning into a fiendish bucking machine. As suddenly as he started he would stop. Then, after a look around him, he would begin to graze again, until some mischievous youngster nipped his quarters, and then the performance would be repeated.

He started to lose his baby coat, and, as the thick hairs fell off, a fine, slick sheen of black became visible, covering his body in a dark mantle; there was not even a white hair on his nose. He was beginning to take more after his sire than his dam. He had inherited his sire's long, sloping shoulder, although his legs showed a fineness which was derived from his dam. He had a nice, short back, with a good length from stifle to hock. His only fault was that he was perhaps a trifle over at the knee.

His character was being moulded, too, in those first few critical months. By nature he was curious, but his curiosity had done nothing but lead him into trouble, and that was beginning to give him a suspicious nature. Coupled with that, he had more fire and temper in him than most of the other foals, perhaps owing to the fact that his dam was a pure thoroughbred.

After five months he had acquired a certain distinction, in that he could outbuck all the other colts and fillies. They would start off in the early morning to get warm and to loosen up. A small group of them raced madly around, then one would fling his heels out, and in a trice they would all be bucking. Heads down, tails switching, backs humped, they would buck wildly until they were tired—all except Fury, who would always be left to buck by himself. By nature he was rather a show-off, as some animals are, and he revelled in having the stage to himself. He would make his leaps and bounds more and more frantic. One day he went too far and crashed down ignominiously on to his nose. His dignity sadly ruffled, he bucked no more that day. But he had soon forgotten the fall, and the next day he was at it again.

One morning his curiosity nearly cost him his young life. Tired and a little bored by the bucking, he ambled away from the main herd and stopped to mouth a piece of grass that took his fancy. The stallion, seeing him wander away, moved slowly and quietly after him.

The foal's attention was suddenly attracted by a movement to his left, and he paused in astonishment. He knew what sticks were, but this was a stick that moved, and it was therefore something new. Something new had to be explored! So he walked over and eyed the snake doubtfully, yet curiously. The black snake reared its head and stared back with its unblinking eyes—still, silent, yet poised, ready to unleash its deadly venom. The black, glittering eyes, the appalling stillness, hypnotized Fury. Then slowly he extended his nose to sniff and find out whether the thing was friend or foe.

There was a flurry of dust, a snort of rage, and he was flung savagely to the ground by his sire's well-aimed kick. The stallion reared high and pounded the weaving snake into a black, pulpy mass on the ground, not satisfied until the dust had mingled with and almost obliterated the snake. Then he turned towards the foal, his eyes blazing with rage at the youngster's stupidity, and moved forward to punish him with teeth and heels.

In one frightened second the foal realized that he had done wrong, and he scrambled to his feet and fled for safety from his sire's wrath. He was too slow, though, and he received such severe punishment that his ardour for exploration was damped for days. Even when the bruises and bites had healed, and his curiosity led him to wander once more, he did not forget the lesson. Snakes were dangerous and never to be sniffed at, only to be killed with the hooves. He also remembered to fear his sire and keep a respectful distance from him.

The first time that he saw a dingo he wanted to push his nose forward to sniff, but the memory of the snake restrained him, and he backed warily away, until his instinct told him that the small, solitary animal could not harm him, if he was strong and well. But he saw what happened to an old mare. Left in the rear by the herd when they moved on for fresh grass, she easily succumbed to the dingoes, and when the herd came that way again, a few weeks later, only bleached bones were left to tell the story.

He saw that he was not the only colt to receive sharp bites from the stallion for wandering, and gradually the colts and fillies took to wandering around together, but always within easy reach of the mares.

The sun was at its highest and hottest point now, and the midday heat sapped the animal's energy so much that bucking became a thing of the past, and most of the day was spent in trying to keep cool, and away from the irritating flies. They would find some water-hole, where they could roll and cover themselves in the protecting mud, but water was becoming increasingly hard to find. The humidity increased daily as the clouds lowered, but the rain still did not come. The sun shone only fitfully through the clouds, and day and night the horses switched their tails in a never-ending battle against the flies.

The grass turned to a sparse brown stuff which, when eaten, did not satisfy their hunger. They began to grow thin, their coats turned dull, and their heads hung low.

One day, though, they sensed the rain—they smelt it in the air. A vivid electrical storm played over the hills in the night, and the distant thunder advanced with ponderous dignity. The clouds banked up low and grey, and it was hard to breathe, so they just stood and suffered, their sides heaving, sweating at the ears, their heads besieged by the flies, their tails moving continuously in a losing battle.

The first raindrop plopped down and disappeared in the dust. Another followed, and then another. Gradually the dust darkened as it absorbed the welcome moisture, and then suddenly the clouds moved, and down came the rain in earnest. Just as suddenly the flies disappeared to those mysterious places that only flies know, and the air became ten degrees colder. The thunder roared and crashed overhead in a magnificent symphony of power and might, accompanying the glory of the rain.

The horses stood there, breathing in the freshness, feeling the dust being washed out of their coats, starting to live again.

That day Fury was just six months old.

CHAPTER TWO

The Round-up

WITH the rain, the bush-land once more changed its sheen from dismal brown to bright green, and as the land changed so did the horses. They fattened out again and showed more life. The colts and fillies returned to their racing and bucking and revelled in life once more.

As the weeks slipped by, marked for the animals by the changes in the movement and appearance of the sun and moon and the gradual changes of the seasons, so did the stallion become more savage. Once a stray two-year-old colt wandered in and challenged the stallion. The herd watched in terrified wonder the quick, brutal defeat of the challenger, and they moved about uneasily as the victorious stallion raced round them, screaming his power and authority.

Fury wondered and watched and wondered again. He was somehow attracted to his sire, but he was afraid of him, afraid of the power of the animal's body, afraid of the magnetism in his eyes, and he warily kept his distance, although he watched and copied the stallion's actions.

As the stallion would stand in the morning, testing the air, so Fury would copy him. He was not sure why he did it; it was enough for him that he copied his sire. So in time the small black colt developed not only a bodily resemblance but also a stance and manner similar to the stallion's, and from a distance he looked just like him. One large and powerful, the other small and puny—they were two of the same kind.

One afternoon Fury was cropping the grass on the slope of the hill where his sire stood on the peak, when, lifting his head, he saw a tenseness in the stallion.

Head high, neck curved in a graceful arch, nostrils flared, the stallion stood perfectly still, like a thing moulded upon the hillside. His eyes glinted and then flamed as he tried to see the object he sought, and detect again the suspicion of the scent that had reached him. He raised and lowered his head, then moved one hoof uneasily. Finding nothing, he turned and trotted down lower and tested the air again. Suddenly he caught the scent, and his nostrils flared. His eyes began to blaze with rage and his heart to pound against his massive chest. Suddenly he saw the horseman.

Now that he had found him he watched and noted. His bush eye, old but sharp, followed every movement the rider and his mount made; then, wheeling suddenly, he cantered down past Fury towards his mares. They felt his agitation and were afraid because of it. The stallion cantered through them, head swinging low, teeth bared against any mare who might oppose him. Turning sharply, he rounded them into a compact bunch, set himself at their head, and cantered away. The mares hastened after their lord; the colts and fillies followed, whinnying their excitement. Ears extended back as he moved onward, the stallion led them away from the rider.

Fury caught a whiff of the pungent man scent and immediately copied his sire. His heart started to thud against his ribs, and he knew he was afraid of that scent, but he did not know why. Never before had he known his sire turn and run from anything; therefore, when he did the danger must be great.

The man did not pursue them. Fury's one quick view of him and the strong, alien scent were stored away in his memory as bad things—things to be wary of and to fear, like the snake. Another lesson was learned.

All the time that he was growing he was learning. Those who did not learn died; nature had no time for the idle or the stupid. The fascination which the stallion had for him was redoubled, and he began to spend more time near him. Grazing just a few yards away, he would watch, look, listen, and learn, and yet at the same time hold himself ready to flee from the stallion's displeasure.

He watched how the stallion tested the air in the morning, he saw how he led the herd to the best water-holes and the choicest grass. He saw how the mares obeyed the stallion, moving where he wanted them to, doing as he commanded. Now and again some recalcitrant mare tried to move away on her own. As soon as the stallion saw what had happened he was after her. There was a flurry of dust and noise, and she would hastily return to the main herd, bitten and sore.

Fury watched the stallion chastise erratic youngsters and scare away the bolder dingoes. His was the fierce, proud spirit which dominated the whole herd. He was always on guard, watching and waiting—always alert; even at night his nostrils and ears moved while, with closed eyes, he stood and slept.

Thus Fury gradually learnt about the responsibilities of the stallion, and he came to appreciate the quality of his leadership, the driving force behind the animal, the work involved, and the obedience and respect that he commanded. To the herd he was not only their lord but also their guardian, and they knew that when danger threatened he was their sole protector.

One hot and dusty day the stallion felt a vague uneasiness which in turn communicated itself to the mares. Instead of spreading out as they grazed, and playing as they roamed around, they were bunched together, watching him. The air was still and unpleasantly hot to breathe, with just a faint, hot wind coming from one direction.

Fury, close to the stallion, watched and copied him when he saw him test the air. Somewhere near at hand was danger, but what danger? Animal danger, fire danger, or man? The stallion as yet could not scent it, but his nerves and instinct had told him that there was danger of some kind, and he anxiously tried to ascertain what it was and from which direction it would come.

Was it a snake or a dingo? Was it caused by other animals? Or was it man? He knew he could fight all animals, but man was the unknown, the doubtful and frightening quantity. His animal cunning and instinct had always told him to flee from men, especially when mounted on other horses.

Many a time the stallion himself had been chased by mounted stockmen attracted by his strength and power, stockmen who wanted to break up the herd which consumed so much of the valuable grass which steers could eat, and also to supplement their own saddle horses. Many a time long ago the stallion had lost mares and foals, but over the years his sagacity and instinct had made him lead the herd away from the haunts of men, and it was many years since one had tried to catch him. He was older now and a little slower, but with age his brain had quickened. He knew more about life; past experiences of being chased had developed his cunning and his confidence in himself.

Restlessly he moved around, wheeling and half rearing in his anxiety; the herd bunched closer together in obedience and waited his commands.

Suddenly the wind changed; raising his head, he caught the scent, only a whiff, but enough to confirm his suspicions, and, with a screech of rage, he placed himself at the head of the herd, ready to gallop off. Fury danced in a frenzy, eyes blazing, as he too suddenly met the man scent coming on the gentle land breeze. It was a hot and dusty breeze, but unmistakably there was the same harsh smell that had made his sire flee the last time.

The stallion cantered up to the hill-top and searched the plain below. He knew there were men down there—and, what was more dangerous, men on horses—but it was not only that which was worrying him. There was something else telling him to beware.

Then suddenly he knew. He both heard and scented at the same time the other men coming in from the rear, coming in against the wind! He cantered down, raced round his mares, placed himself at the lead, and moved off. Tails high in the air, steps short and sharp, the herd swept away, snorting with alarm. Fury found himself cantering beside his dam again. It seemed quite natural to return to her side when such danger appeared.

Leaving the hills, the stallion increased his pace, intending to get well away from the riders, but the other men had now closed in, and gradually the herd was forced in one direction. The stallion's flanks were covered with the white froth of exertion and fear, he neighed shrilly and then burst into a full gallop. The whole herd, thoroughly alarmed now, blindly followed him and tried to out-distance the riders.

Ears well back, heads low and extended, with the thick dust rising around them, they flew over the plain, jumping small gullies and fallen trees and swerving round the larger ones, their hooves making a rumble like low and distant thunder. The stallion was frantically trying to get his herd ahead of the riders, but although he himself had the speed, the mares were slowed down by the younger animals and the late foals.

The buildings of a cattle station appeared in the distance, and the stallion made an effort to break away to one side. His mares flew after him in blind faith, but the men at the flanks closed in, their whips cracking and their voices raised in shouts, and the animals swung back again in terror.

Suddenly the stallion saw a gap. He thrust himself forward even faster and was through, past the outriders. There was a hoarse shout, and two men galloped madly after him, but the stallion, unburdened by any weight on his back, easily outpaced them. Two mares followed, but the rest were quickly turned back.

Fury had started the gallop glorying in the excitement and in the use of his strong young limbs and surplus energy, but those young limbs were not used to such a hard pace, and gradually he fell back to the rear with the older mares and youngest foals. His small mind was now racing with terror at the nearness of the riders, and his heart pounded painfully, but, try as he might, he could not increase his pace any more.

Eyes wide with terror, he stumbled and then fell heavily, twisting his neck as a horse will to save it from being broken. The rest of the herd and riders thundered past in a vast, dust-laden cloud of noise and fear and then receded into the hazy distance.

Fury scrambled to his feet, turned round, and cantered off after his vanishing sire. His long legs faltered with the effort and strain until gradually his pace became a slow walk. His head hung low, his tail drooped miserably, and he was conscious that for the first time in his young life he was quite alone, and he was afraid.

He spent the night standing by a ring-barked tree—standing alone, but listening. His ears moved backward and forward, trying to pick up the faintest sound of other horses. The moon shone over the now quiet plain, glistening on the bark of the old tree until it seemed to be made of silver. The tall, naked branches beckoned to the sky like a giant's hand. It was a long night, and Fury heard and saw nothing. Not even a dingo or a rabbit moved, not a wallaby or a snake. The only sound came from the frenzied whining of the mosquitoes.

The sun rose in the morning, and by noon the next day was a fiery red ball, sending down stabbing fingers of flame. The heat waves shimmered and danced away out to the horizon; Fury stamped a hoof, and a tiny cloud of dust wafted into his nostrils.

He was lonely. No longer could he gallop with the others or indulge in frenzies of wild bucking. He lifted his head high and whinnied shrilly, but only an echo mocked back at him. He lowered his head and idly lipped a few pieces of grass. He spent the next night under the same tree, recovering his strength; then, when the sun rose again, he started to move slowly back towards the hills.

He took his time, stopping now and again to eat and drink. There was no sire now to chase him around and no young colts to tantalize him; his whole time now was spent in moving onward and looking for something to eat and drink.

As the days passed there was less and less water at the water-holes. Back once more in the hills his memory of events began to fade. He had not the mind of a man, to recall events at will —though present facts could remind him of past ones. What he most relied on now was his instinct. His mother was forgotten. Even the terror of the round-up vanished from his mind when there was nothing left to remind him of it. But he was always conscious of his loneliness. He did not forget other horses, and he was always on the look-out for them.

The weeks turned into months, and in his wanderings over the hills he came to know every track and creek and—most important of all—every water-hole. He scrambled up steep slopes and stood on them, looking out, as he had seen the stallion do, but always the scene was the same—a harsh, dry, sun-burnt land, with no sign of movement, dead and still.

He found places where he could get down to have a roll in thick mud or dust. He also found himself suitable trees and rocks where he could scratch his mane and tail to his heart's delight. He lost completely the gangling, baby look. His body thickened and grew in proportion to his legs, which in turn filled out, and slowly his proportions became those of a horse. His neck acquired some of the thickness and his steps some of the sureness of a full-grown horse. His whinny became more harsh and brassy. He was growing up, and becoming aware of who and what he was. His was a wide, interesting world now— far beyond a foal's understanding.

All through his wanderings he neither saw nor scented another horse. Once from one of his lofty peaks he caught sight of things moving in the distance, but when he saw that they were riders he felt fear again, a fear that came suddenly with the memory of the round-up. He trembled and fled. His dignity all gone, he turned and raced frantically back to where he thought he was safe—back to the hills which held peace and quiet for him. Here at least he could feel free.

So he came to recognize men as dreaded enemies, to be avoided at all costs. He must always keep distance between himself and them. Men were bad; men brought fear and terror, dust and noise. The dread of them must never be forgotten.

So in his animal mind he reasoned—not as we do, but slowly and surely. He learnt these things as he had learnt from the stallion's nips and bites that snakes were bad. There was no one to tell him now, but, if he did not learn, nature would not let him survive. It was a learning by instinct and by trial and error.

He would climb to the top of a hill or slope and stand there for hours, head high in the air, mane whipping and blowing in the breeze, nostrils extended, searching, always searching for others of his kind. Then suddenly he would grow tired of it all and come bounding down the slope, leaping over the rocks until, just as the land levelled out, he would drop his head and treat himself to a short, sharp, exhilarating outburst of bucking. Then just as suddenly he would stop and begin to graze. Pushing the grass with his delicate lips, nipping the blades which took his fancy, he would slowly and gratefully munch it up, then once more majestically climb the slope.

Always he was searching. Once he had seemed undisturbed by the lack of horses, but as time passed the yearning inside him became stronger, for horses are gregarious and friendly animals. Sometimes he would stand and neigh shrilly, and the echoes of his own voice would make him toss his head up and down with dissatisfaction at the emptiness of it all.

There was very little life of any kind in the hills. Fury knew that a large eagle had its eyrie amid some rough crags, and near the foot of one of the hills he had seen an old-man kangaroo with his mates and a few joeys. He had stared in amazement when he first saw the joeys fly to the safety of their mothers' pouches, while the red kangaroo had thumped the ground with his thick tail in warning. Then they had all vanished, sailing over the ground in fantastic leaps, their huge tails thumping down to propel them forward as their strong hind-legs lifted their bodies.

One night he had been vaguely disturbed by an alien sound. He could smell something strange, and his ears twitched as he strove to identify it. Then, his curiosity overcoming his suspicion, he went to investigate.

It was not a dark night, the moon was well up, and he could see a small glow in the distance. He walked towards it, nostrils moving at many unfamiliar sounds. Then suddenly again came the weird noise and he leapt to one side, snorting and blowing his alarm. Then, when nothing happened, he moved cautiously on again towards the flames of the camp fire.

The small group of aborigines squatting in front of their fire completely ignored him. One of them blew the harsh-booming didgeridoo, which set him trembling, while the man scent—although this time different—made his flesh squirm. Yet for some reason he stayed, fascinated. Then one young buck got up to do a primitive dance. This was too much for Fury, and he turned and fled. For hours afterwards he was disturbed by the sounds of the walkabout party, and he trotted off uneasily into the night.

He started to wander down and away from his hills, out far to the west, to land which was new to him, land which was more thickly covered with trees, gums, wattles, and paper-barks, their branches so close together at times that the bright blue sky was completely hidden overhead. Between the trees he found some grass which still held greenness, although the trees around were dry and brittle. The barren pieces of ground were brown and full of large cracks as a result of the drought, but the land seemed different to him, and, as it seemed different, he enjoyed himself as he explored.

CHAPTER THREE

Fire

FIFTY miles away to the west, across the sparsely treed plain, two dingoes started a fight over a buck rabbit which one of them had killed. It had been another hot day, and the dingo had patiently stalked the rabbit and finally killed it on a pile of loose stones.

Challenged, he froze into immobility, then, drawing back his lips, he snarled at the intruder. They closed in battle, slashing and gouging with their teeth, rolling through the trees up a pile of near-by stones. Still snapping and feinting, they closed again, and one dislodged a stone. It fell from the pile, dropped down among the trees, and struck another stone. A spark shot off at a tangent and landed in a pile of long, dry grass. At the same moment the wind moved, and the spark glowed red against a dried grass frond, which spluttered and then burst into flame. The flame ran joyously up the frond, consumed it, and then dropped down again to burn among the grass. The wind began to blow harder, and the tiny fire moved forward.

At first only weak, the fire gathered strength as it ate its way through the brittle grass and fallen twigs and began to climb the dry tree-trunks, aided by the wind. The two dingoes stopped fighting, looked at the fire, and fled, leaving the rabbit's carcass to burn.

The wind increased, and the fire sprang up, strong and powerful, advancing straight through the trees, leaving a wake of death and destruction. And the wind blew even stronger.

Fury stood in the shade of a tree, dozing in the hot sun's rays, his tail switching against the mosquitoes which buzzed around. Underfoot the grass was pale-brown and had very little value as food, but the trees were cool and restful.

For no apparent reason Fury opened his eyes and lifted his head, with his ears pricked as he listened, but he heard nothing. A vague feeling of uneasiness overtook him, but the only sounds that he could hear were the usual bush noises: the chirping of the crickets, the whine of the mosquitoes, and the occasional screech of a parakeet.

A wallaby jumped out of the trees, swerved at the sight of him, and then continued on his way. A few seconds later another one followed, then a large buck rabbit shot past, with its white tail bobbing.

Fury was really uneasy now. Something was disturbing the other denizens of the bush, and he did not know what it was. He moved his feet uneasily and listened again, every nerve straining. There were other movements in the bush now, and more animals moved forward, all going in the same direction. He snorted, and his instinct told him to follow them, but his curiosity made him wait to see what the enemy was.

He looked long and hard in the direction from which the animals had come and thought he heard something. A sudden movement made him start and then rear in blinding terror, and he came down, lashing with his forelegs at the snake under his feet. The reptile squirmed out of the way and passed on at an astonishing speed after the other creatures.

Fury blew and snorted, then trotted in an uneasy circle.

Stopping, he listened again, and this time his keen ears picked out an odd, disturbing sound. He did not look up—animals rarely do—but if he had he would have seen the smoke of the fire drifting over the sky, blocking out the sun as if wafted over the tree-tops.

Trotting a few more paces, he halted and nervously snatched at a twig; he mouthed it for a second, then let it drop. The sound was nearer now and very plain. Peering through the trees, he could see something moving, something of a frightening, fantastic shape, that crackled, snapped, hissed, and roared. Fury felt stark terror. It was not the fear that he felt for the stallion, nor the fear that he felt for man, but a new, indefinable fear. His body shuddered; then he turned and trotted rapidly through the trees.

He threaded his way delicately past the strong trunks, bu tdid not hurry yet. He was leaving the fear behind him, so why should he hurry? He was not to know that a bush fire sometimes spreads more quickly through tree-tops than over the ground, and that bush fires tend to form a circle if driven hard by the wind. And the wind *was* increasing. It was only when a burning branch fell on to his quarters, singeing his tail at the top, that he realized his danger, and by then it was nearly too late.

He tried to extend his pace, but the trees were still thick, and he could go no faster than a canter. The fire crackled angrily behind him, moving in quick spurts as it found some particularly dry piece of wood. Grass went up in a sudden yellow sheet of flame, the branches of the trees crackled and shot off hot sparks which in turn started other fires, and in command was the wind, driving and urging onward, until the fire advanced inexorably like a tide, revelling in its deadly rampage.

Fury felt the heat from the flames and, panic-stricken, tried

to go faster. He blundered over a fallen tree-trunk, crashing to
the earth. Something burning fell on his mane, and the pain
drove him to his feet. He plunged wildly forward, eyes staring
in terror, ears straining back, listening to the fire. His legs
moved as fast as the terrain would allow them. Another branch
dropped; leaping aside, he crashed into the trunk of a tree and
bounded off with his sides badly bruised. In a mad panic now,
he tried to gallop through everything in front of him. He flung
himself against the trees, trampling the smaller ones down with
his weight and bouncing off the larger ones.

Ahead of him was the flat grassland, but now it was barred
by a blazing red and yellow curtain, a thing that moved backward and forward, reaching out to take everything in, leaping
up to grasp the heavens, darting both sideways and downward.
It was everywhere—the curtain of fire!

Fury reared to a standstill, snorting and blowing his fear,
dancing on his hind-legs. Cinders dropped on him as he plunged
to get out of their reach, the air was hot and thin, and it was
hard to breathe properly. The smoke was lowering, and his eyes
had begun to smart. The ground was hot under his hooves. He
tried to dance away from the pain, but it was the same everywhere. The shimmering red and yellow was still ahead.

For the second time in his life Fury was very near to death.
The curtain of fire in front was not a thick one, but it would
not be long before other fingers of fire joined up with it, and
then the way would be impassable.

Fury was nearly mad with fear by now. His eyes stood out
of their sockets as if they would burst. His mane was tangled
with twigs and smuts. Cinders had dropped all over his body
and mingled with the sweat of fear and heat. Pieces of the trees
through which he had blundered stuck in his tail and around his

fetlocks. His right leg had been torn and lacerated almost down to the cannon bone by a tree which had failed to yield to him. The fire was nearly up to him, the heat from behind singeing him and making him jump frantically. A few hairs on the bottom of his tail had started to smoulder, more pieces of cinder were glowing in his mane, and suddenly a very large branch fell with a thud across his back. The shock and the pain of his burning coat were too much for him, and he leapt straight into the burning curtain to escape. Three huge bounds, and he was out, racing as fast as he could over the long, tinder-dry grass, away from the incandescent trees, back to the only place which meant quietness and safety—his beloved hills.

The fire surged after him like a monster deprived of his prey, but, hard and demanding as it was, Fury was quicker. Driven by a terror that he had never known before, he unleashed himself into a gallop which soon put the rapidly moving fire far behind him.

His terror had almost turned his brain, and at this point he was not quite normal. When he could gallop no longer he swung back into a trot, then into a walk, and finally shuddered to a halt. His mad flight had extinguished the many small fires on his coat and tail. He shuddered from head to hoof and could go no farther. His limbs ached with his many cuts, burns, and bruises, which became more painful as he cooled off. Behind, he could see the fire turning in a fresh direction with the change of the wind, and he knew now that he was safe. His leg was sore, and his off forefoot was split at the toe. Some small stones had worked their way up the split, and the foot was very tender. He was a very unhappy animal.

That night the fire fizzled out when the wind died down and could no longer stir up the flames. and as the trees and grass had thinned out there was nothing for the fire to devour, so, unable to quench its appetite, the monster reluctantly died.

Fifty miles away to the west two hungry dingoes again fought to decide which of them should eat a dead bandicoot!

Fury spent the night near some rocks. He was too sore to lie down, and his foot was far too painful for him to move far, but he was a young, healthy animal, and after two more days he had almost forgotten the fire, except when some sharp stone touched his split hoof and reminded him.

Another enemy was thus filed away in his mind with man, the stallion, and snakes. As the stones worked themselves out and the foot began to heal and draw together again, he moved on to his hills and to the safe, familiar land. Fright and terror always came to him when he was away from them, and it was only when he was once more amid their gum-treed, gaunt, and barren slopes that he relaxed.

As before, time passed uneventfully, and as it did, so Fury grew. His body filled out, and his neck curved and thickened. His tail became a splendid banner, and his eyes were hard and fierce. He was not a baby colt any longer, but a well-grown yearling, a young horse, swift and strong from living and fighting strenuously in the wild bush-land.

It was a long, dry summer that year—one of the hardest in the memory of living man, so the stockmen and outriders said. The rains failed to come at the right time, and the ground began to crack and dry. It was a hard and cruel land, a land which knew no mercy, which could never be fully tamed, but only subdued with water. And when the water did not come, when the rains failed, then the land cracked and split, as if laughing at those who tried to live on it.

The precious water-holes changed into soggy morasses; then the mud dried out until all that was left in the earth was a cracked brown hollow. Seeds dropped on the hard earth and lay there dormant, waiting for moisture to swell them into growth. As the earth dried up in the bush, life began to die. The wandering steers drifted back to the cattle stations. Gaunt and emaciated, the weak, the sick, and the old plodded slowly, with heads low and still tails, to where water used to be, and when they got there and found none they would stand, moaning pitifully, and then drop and die.

Those that died quickly were the lucky ones. They were not to know the excruciating pain of having their eyes pulled from the sockets by carrion birds. Nor did they feel the savage teeth of the dingoes tearing the still living flesh away from their weak limbs. Those that died quickly were the lucky ones.

A feeling of death began to hang over the land, for life had begun to vanish.

Fury was growing thin. His ribs stood out, and his coat no longer showed the bright shine of health, but the dull pallor of a hungry and thirsty animal. His eyes began to stand out from his face as the flesh disappeared. No longer were his spirits like quicksilver; his confidence in life had left him. Alone and suspicious of everything, he walked slowly along, looking for something to drink and some grass to eat, that he too might live and not die.

He passed out of the hills into the valley on the far side, into a land which was new to him. Here, though, things were just the same. As far as he could see there was dry brown earth, with just a few odd fronds of bleached grass standing upright. Nothing moved, because very little lived. Even the ants and the beetles seemed to have taken refuge against the heat, waiting for the rain.

Fury moved onward, driven by the desire to drink. He had tried to chew branches, but there was no moisture there, and even when he moved the stones he found only red, barren earth beneath them. As he moved on he came upon many white, bleached bones—grim landmarks, and inescapable reminders of a land held in the grip of a drought.

Fury went on, driven by some force inside him. He knew that if he stayed in one place he would die, but his progress was slow and made with great effort. His eyes had become dull, and his head hung low, as he moved onward, always searching for water. The powerful, basic life force, the will to live, kept him going. He was in strange and new territory, but he ignored it all, his whole being concentrated on the search for water!

As the sun started its descent he paused and lifted his head. A faint, teasing smell reached him—a smell that stirred his dulled mind, quickened his blood, and made him lift his feet with more care. Yes, there it was again. Coming over on the evening land-breeze was the smell of water.

He lifted his head high and started to trot towards the smell. It was the broken, unsteady trot of a half-starved, nearly dead animal, but it *was* a trot. His limbs tired easily, but his thoroughbred spirit and willpower drove him on. He stumbled and nearly fell; then, as the smell became stronger, he broke into a ragged canter, his head high. Where was it, this strong, beautiful smell of water?

Breasting a rise, he saw it—a small, muddy patch of earth and water beneath a clump of eucalyptus trees. He whipped himself into a faster canter and slithered down towards the water, feet splaying out clumsily. Somehow he kept his balance and suddenly he was there, wading in to drink the thick, muddy, brackish-tasting water. He wallowed in the sucking mud, lowered his head, and drank greedily. The stinking, stagnant water tasted unbelievably sweet to him. Mouthful upon mouthful he eagerly gulped down, but then nature warned him to stop. Too much water after no water at all, and he would get colic. So he lowered his head, plunged his nose in, and blew in delight; then he slowly collapsed on to the mud and treated himself to the luxury of a roll. It was an ungainly roll, and it took a lot of energy, but when he scrambled upright again he was already a different horse. Moreover, he now had a very good protection against the flies.

He looked around. The clump of eucalyptus trees provided some shade, and he was grateful for that. Then he noticed something else, something he had not seen for a long time. Stretching away from the foot of the trees was a stretch of green grass, short and coarse perhaps, but still green grass! The small spring which had fed the water-hole throughout the drought had seeped to the surface of the earth farther out, and produced a strip of emerald green in the barren land.

Fury clambered out of the mud and started to pull hungrily at the grass, tearing at it with his strong front teeth, chewing in haste until his hunger was satisfied. Then, in bodily content for the first time in many weeks, he flung his head up and tested the air in his old manner—and he had a shock.

For coming towards him on the night air was a smell which he had not scented for nearly a year. Horses! He raised his head and whinnied shrilly, and over the air came an exciting response. He flung out his tail, arched his thin neck, and trotted with some of his old arrogance towards the sound. His gait was

not that of the proud animal of the past months, but it still had
a certain aristocratic majesty.

The moon had risen, and suddenly he saw a sight that made
him dig his toes in and halt abruptly. The old fear came flood-
ing back with painful memories, and he stood in confusion. For
before him stood his sire and two mares.

They stared back at him in equal amazement; then the old
stallion flung his head up and down uncertainly, and the mares
nickered boldly at the intruder.

Fury waited nervously. He knew that he should be afraid of
his sire, and in a way he was, but his joy at meeting his own
kind again was greater than his fear, and greater than the other
vague, uneasy feeling which was flitting through his mind, and
which he did not yet quite understand.

The stallion lifted his head high, flung his tail out, and trotted
towards his son with stiff, jerky paces. He halted, and the two
animals regarded each other, a yard apart. The stallion looked
at the image of himself: the same glorious blackness, the arrogant head carriage, the proud head and fierce eye, the body
which, though thin, showed muscles under the skin—muscles
and bones which had not yet finished growing.

They touched noses and blew. Then, squealing a warning,
the stallion reared. Fury wheeled to one side and paused. Here
was the companionship which he had craved over the many
long months, and he did not want to lose it, but he was not a
strong animal, and he knew that if he fought the stallion now
he would die under those large, flailing hooves.

The vague, uneasy feeling had defined itself, and he looked
long and hard towards the mares. He too was a stallion in the
making, and he stared back at his sire. The stallion suddenly
lunged and snapped, showing his yellow fighting teeth. They

left a welt on Fury's skin, and Fury swung round defiantly, ready to lash out with his heels. Then the knowledge came to him that he was not strong enough to fight yet. His long starvation had left him weak, and his reflexes were slow. He lashed out with his heels, but the stallion swerved easily and quickly bowled Fury on to the earth.

Fury scrambled on the ground, saw the stallion's descending hoof, rolled over, and jumped to his feet and fled, with the stallion in pursuit. Completely gone were pride and dignity, he was hurt both in body and in mind. Even the companionship of his own kind was denied to him, but as he galloped away he realized that one day he would not run—one day he too would be strong and fierce, and then he would stand and fight. By attacking and chasing him the stallion acknowledged him as a rival. In those few fleeting seconds Fury finally left colthood behind and became a horse.

He fled back to the water and the trees, knowing that the stallion would soon go back to his mares. He was aware now of the difference in himself. He would have liked the company of the mares; but though it was desirable now, later on it would be a necessity. Soon it would be time for him to have his own mares—to guard them, to lead them, and to reproduce his kind. Nature had almost made her full circle.

CHAPTER FOUR

The Rider

H E wandered back to the hills and was lucky enough to find grass and muddy water, but still the heat seared the land. During the day he stood motionless, under a tree or rock—anywhere which would give him shade; during the night he hunted for food and precious water.

One morning he noticed something strange in the sky, something from so far back in the past that he had almost forgotten it: a few wisps of clouds flitted over the horizon, white, frothy parcels of tantalizing lace. He watched them linger on the rim of the sky and then move slowly towards him. Slowly the clouds piled up, turning from delicate white to an uneasy, deep-grey blanket, and with them came humidity. The sun vanished above the clouds, and now the land sweltered, sweated, and waited. For a whole day the clouds hung there, low and ominous in the sky, and the wind dropped. All sounds of life ceased, the flies disappeared, the mosquitoes vanished, and there was a frightening hush over the barren and dying land.

As darkness came, a single jagged finger of lightning stabbed and rent the sky in rage; there was a moment of silence, and then the thunder bellowed and the rain came. It came not in a steady stream, but in one of the blinding deluges so common in that country. All the months of thirsting were appeased, as the raindrops lashed and rent the brown soil, churning and mixing it into a deep mud, swelling and bursting the dormant seeds, giving the land, man, and beast the command to live again.

Fury stood with his quarters to the rain, his head low. The raindrops stung and bit into his many sores and bruises, but he did not move. He stood there and relished the clean feeling of the water, the delight in breathing freely again, and the knowledge of plenty to eat and drink.

The rain continued all that night and most of the next day. It stopped for a few hours the next evening, and Fury ate and drank. Then it began to rain again, and continued to rain for three whole weeks; then it stopped as suddenly as it had started.

The earth was sodden, but the air was clean, fresh, and wholesome, and the terrible, racking heat had disappeared. The thousands of grass seeds had germinated, shooting down myriads of tiny, hair-like roots, until one morning a sheen of green velvet danced over the land, stretching to the horizon. The frogs appeared and started their long, deep-voiced melodies, and the crickets disappeared. Everywhere was life. Animal and plant were living and growing again, taking full advantage of the rain before the sun in the course of the cycle of nature should dry up the land once more.

Fury ate and drank well. Slowly the flesh came back on to his frame. His coat began to thicken and shine, and his neck arched proudly. He was more than two years old now. Far behind were the battles, the trials, and the tribulations of his babyhood. He would still grow in stature, but his character and spirit were formed and would never alter any further now.

He stood sixteen hands, and would probably make seventeen by the time he had finished growing. He had the small feet of a thoroughbred, but in everything else he took after his sire, and his body betokened strength and power. His movements were oiled and strong—almost effortless—and he carried his body with grace and joy. His well-formed head, with its concave nose, hinted at a trace of the Arab somewhere far back in his ancestry. His eyes were set well apart and shone with fearlessness and intelligence. His ears were small—again a hint of the Arab—and he carried them erect and sharp. His head bent well at the poll, and was supported by the thick, powerful neck muscles of a stallion.

Although he had small feet, they were well formed, and there was plenty of bone and substance in his legs. His bent over-knees were broad and flat, and it was probably this defect which helped to give him his great speed over the rough terrain of the bush. He could throw his knees just that fraction more forward than the average horse, and because of his wild life he was absolutely sound in the legs. The tendons stood out taut, like cords, and his hocks were beautifully straight and unblemished. His quarters were big and broad, without being ugly, and the line of his body, from stifle down to the hock, was long and very strong. Hence his hind-legs could be driven forward with a longer reach than normal.

His bodily make-up was almost that of a race-horse, but the muscles, big and strong, which stood out all over him, showed him for what he really was—a bush stallion.

Fury had forgotten about his bucking habits, until one morning, as he went up to a tree to rub his tail against it, an opossum moved suddenly in the branches. He was so shocked that he whipped round and indulged in a frenzy of bucking, and found delight in loosening some of the tension in his muscles. So once more it became a habit for him to buck early in the morning, to loosen himself, and to warm his blood when the wind was chilly.

One morning, as the sun started its climb, his keen ears heard something, a sound that was strange to him, and, following his old habit, he climbed the sloping ground to find a vantage-point from which to look over the land. At the same moment that Fury reached the top of the slope, the rider reined in his horse and smiled to himself, then rode on again in Fury's direction.

Fury stood for a second, then turned and cantered down the slope. His mind churned over the warnings and lessons of the past: "Beware of man, any man, but of a man on a horse most of all." He suddenly remembered the noise and the horror of the round-up and the loneliness afterwards, and his heart began to beat violently. Acknowledging his enemy's presence, he turned and fled. He cantered away from the hills with short, jerky steps, tail waving in the air, snorting his alarm. His whole body was coiled like a spring, but he was not yet ready to unleash himself into a wild gallop. After a while he stopped to listen. He could not see the rider, but he could both hear and scent him as he moved steadily nearer.

Fury moved on and for the rest of the day kept a safe distance between himself and the sound of the pursuing rider. At times he cantered swiftly, and when he stopped the sounds would be lost, but after a while his sharp ears would pick out the metallic *click-click* of hooves on stones, slowly but surely following him. All that day he was followed, and, no matter how hard he tried, he could never rid himself of his pursuer. He tried various paces over different types of ground, but although he might elude his enemy for a time, sooner or later the rider would draw nearer.

It was the same during the night. The moon came up bright and early, and when normally he would have grazed and rested

Acknowledging his enemy's presence, he turned and fled

he spent the time anxiously listening and moving on. He became agitated and wasted time and energy in trotting backward and forward, while the rider steadily came nearer on his own fit and corn-fed horse.

All through the next day and on towards the evening the slow chase continued. Fury was working himself into a state of nervous exhaustion. He had not the mind to realize that, with his speed, he could safely get away from the rider—that he could safely take his time eating and drinking. To keep a distance between him and the man was now an obsession, and so, with the lack of food and water, his great strength began to wane. He wasted time listening when he should have eaten; he wasted more time aimlessly wandering around when he could have galloped away to freedom. His animal mind was unable to decide sensibly what should be done. All he knew was that there was danger, and that he must not relax his vigilance. He stood still, only his ears and nostrils moving, only his raised tail and staring eyes denoting his worry and fear.

But at last he had to eat and drink. His body demanded this attention, and so he found a small spring with some choice grass round it. His hunger and thirst made him forget his caution for a few minutes, and when the wind veered round, taking the scent of the man away from him, he did not notice. There was to be no further warning of danger; nature accepted no excuse for his weakness now. He had failed her.

Fury lifted his head and, to his horror, heard the rush of hoof-beats right behind him. He leapt forward into a wild gallop, but it was too late, and something rough and harsh settled round his neck. He accelerated, and then crashed heavily to the ground as the rope tightened. He grunted heavily and scrambled madly to his feet, trying to plunge forward again—away from the rider and the vicious thing round his neck. The rope bit sharp and deep, and once more he crashed heavily to the earth. The rope slackened, and this encouraged him to try to escape again, but once more he fell—this time very heavily—and he winded himself. The rider's trained horse had eased back, intelligently taking the strain of the rope on the saddle's pommel and bracing his forelegs.

Fury scrambled to his feet again, his sides heaving. His whole instinct told him to flee and fight the thing around his neck, but his brain told him that three times he had tried this and three times he had fallen, hurting himself and lowering his dignity. So he stood trembling with emotion, not knowing what to do. His ears were damp with the sweat of fear, his eyes staring, and his nostrils extended, as they blew sounds of distrust. His heart pounded painfully, as his mind tried to puzzle everything out. He wanted to devote his whole attention to the man, and also to the thing on his neck. So he compromised: he kept his eyes on the man, and his ears flat back, listening to the rope.

The man sat on his horse and started to talk to him—strange, harsh sounds—while he patted the neck of his own mount, all the time keeping the rope straight and taut.

Fury shuddered and flinched at the closeness of the man and at the discordant noise of his voice. He watched the other horse in amazement and disgust, as he put an ear back to acknowledge a pat on his neck—apparently liking the gesture. The thought of a man being so close to him filled Fury's being with such intense, blinding horror that he suddenly plunged and frantically fought the rope. Then, finding that it would not give, he reared and lashed with his forelegs. He lost his balance and found himself falling for the fourth time. Then the earth crashed against his withers and back, and he lay helpless and stunned. The man swore to himself. His mount stood quietly, rather astonished at all the fuss, his ears moving backward and forward as he waited for fresh instructions from his rider.

Fury came to, his head buzzing painfully, and his ribs hurting. He found it hard to breathe. He was very frightened, not with the fear that he had felt for the snake—that could be killed —or the stallion—that could be fought one day—but with a new, overwhelming, indescribable fear. Nothing like this had ever happened to him before, and he did not know what to do. He put his forelegs out and cautiously hauled himself erect. His legs wobbled like a foal's.

The man watched him anxiously; he had once seen a wild horse twist its guts in falling backward. He kept on talking in a low, soft drone, saying any silly thing, but never pausing. He knew full well the power and implications of the human voice, and the terror that a sudden change in it could bring to an animal. He knew, too, that his voice, because of its strangeness, was harsh and frightening to this wild, untamed horse.

"Easy, fella, I'm not going to hurt you. We're going to get to know each other. I've seen you often before and I reckon it's high time some one laid a claim on you, you black Fury."

Fury's legs steadied themselves, and he stopped trembling a little. He did not know what to do. He could not gallop away; he had tried that and each time had suffered the pain and humiliation of falling. And when he reared he only hurt himself, so that was no good. He stood there and tried to puzzle the matter out. His whole instinct and being told him to fight and fight and fight, but his common sense told him that it was useless. This man was his enemy—that he knew. But what was he to do? He tensed his muscles and waited, eyeing the man and the other horse. The horse stood there placidly, his ears flickering, all the time watching and waiting for further commands from his rider.

The man's voice droned on; it never stopped, its tone never altered. To Fury it did not seem quite so harsh now, and he thought he caught something comforting in it. Then the man moved in the saddle, and again Fury felt only terror and fear. He struggled frantically against the rope, but as it bit deeply into his neck and started to choke him, he stopped. He had the sense to realize that the more he struggled against the rope the more it could hurt him, whereas when he stood quite still there was no pain.

The man and the wild animal eyed each other. Then the man very slowly and carefully dismounted, leaving the rope still fastened to the saddle horn; the trained stock-horse kept the rope taut.

Seeing the man standing away from his mount filled Fury with fresh terror. He had always associated man with horses and had never really imagined him on his own; on his own man seemed even more terrifying. Fury backed a step, then remembered the rope and stood still again. Already he was learning, and the man noted it with a smile. The man walked over to a gum-tree and whistled his mount over. The intelligent animal stepped daintily across, still keeping the strain on the rope. Fury leant back and then stood still again, waiting and watching. For a few seconds there was a tug-of-war between the two animals, but the pain of the biting rope made Fury give in.

The man waited for his mount to reach his side, then he reached up and started to untie the rope. He worked quickly and quietly, not talking now. Then in one swift movement he

whipped the rope off the saddle and around a low branch of
the tree. Fury jumped at the same time. He had been watching
the man closely, but he was not quite quick enough. By the
time he had lunged the rope was around the branch twice, and,
by straining back, he only hurt himself again. The man, satisfied
that the rope was safely tied and high enough to prevent the
stallion getting a leg over it, led his own horse away and made
camp.

He neither looked at Fury nor showed any interest in him,
and this gave Fury time to settle himself down and watch him.
As long as he was not near him he thought he was safe. The
man tied his own horse, after feeding him; then he lit himself
a small fire, boiled a billy of tea, and ate some dampers. Finally
he rolled a cigarette, lay down, and listened to the bush night
life.

Fury watched, but as the man did nothing to hurt him he
allowed his tense muscles to relax and even lowered his head
to snatch a mouthful of grass. He kept the rope fairly taut
around his neck, not having the sense to move a step nearer the
man and ease the strain, so he had to eat with his legs firmly
braced, and he could not manage very well. At last it entered
his head that he must move another step nearer to the man in
order to get his head low enough to be able to eat properly.
He did so, and so learnt another lesson. The man lying by the
fire grinned to himself.

It seemed a long night to Fury, but for the man it was short.
The deriding laugh of an early kookaburra woke him, and he
yawned. He crawled out of his blanket, moved his pillow—the
upturned saddle—and stood up.

Fury instantly alerted himself, and regarded the man dubiously. The man made a fire and put the billy on again, had his

breakfast—again damper—then thoroughly soused the fire with earth and walked towards his horse, carrying the saddle and bridle. Fury watched, as the man swiftly saddled his horse and led the animal over towards the gum-tree. Another one of those quick movements, and the rope had been untied and was once more fastened to the saddle. Lightly holding the reins, the man slipped into the saddle, and the rope tightened as the horse backed away and awaited fresh orders.

Fury felt the rope tighten and reared in protest. He came down, lashing with his forelegs. The man turned his horse, nudged with his heels, and moved away. The rope tightened unbearably, and Fury had to move—or choke.

He obeyed the rope and moved. He plunged forward, wildly fighting to break the rope and jerking his head from side to side, but the steady movement of the rider tightened the rope again, and the searing pain in Fury's throat forced him to desist and follow. Then he leapt again, this time to one side. The rope tightened, and he fell, but he was back on his feet instantly—fighting, plunging, and tearing in rage.

All the time the man kept his mount steadily walking forward.

There was a vicious, burning, tearing pain in Fury's neck; and though the mad desire to fight was still there, his predominant good sense told him to calm down and wait. There would be time to fight later; he could *not* stand this searing pain. "Be wary of the rope, but wait your chance," his mind said. He obeyed, and followed the rider. He kept at the extreme end of the rope and allowed himself to be hauled along. It was a tiring day for him. Although it was not the hot season, by the middle of the day his black coat was covered with a white froth, and his sides heaved. The fact that he had not eaten

properly during the chase had weakened him considerably. By
nightfall they had not travelled more than twenty miles.
The rider's mount was still fresh, but Fury was quiet with
tiredness.

When the man pitched camp he tied Fury as before, letting
him stay near water and feed this time. He went through the
same performance as the previous night, taking no chances with
the wild stallion.

Fury was tired and submissive that night, but even then he
did not relax his vigilance, and he watched the man continually.
Every move that the man made was studied by two large,
anxious eyes. Fury was unable to understand how the other
horse could suffer the man near him, let alone obey him. It hurt
his confidence in his own kind and made him even more
suspicious of the man. That night he was a very puzzled, foot-
sore, and weary animal.

He did not try to fight the rope the next day, and when the
man ignored him he followed quietly enough. By deliberately
ignoring Fury the man knew he was giving him time to
analyse and learn his scent. His quiet, unhurried movements
would not startle the stallion's tense spirit, and as he knew no
animal—especially a wild one—liked to be stared at he studi-
ously avoided even looking in Fury's direction.

It took five long, hard days to reach the station, moving at
such a slow pace. Fury gradually accepted his rôle of following
at the end of the rope, although his spirit ordered him to fight
when he went through and past his beloved hills. But although
his spirit gave the order, his body was too tired and weak to
obey. Throughout the journey he remained tense and cautious,
waiting for the man to make a mistake. One slip by the man,
and Fury would snatch his freedom. But the man was wise in

the ways of horses, and he made no mistake. His craftiness far outweighed Fury's animal cunning.

At noon on the fifth day the buildings of the station came into view, shimmering through the dust, and the man sighed his pleasure and patted his mount's neck.

"Nearly there, old son. It's been quite a trip," he mused.

As they neared the station buildings so Fury became more agitated. He receded to the farthest extent of the rope, to keep himself as far as possible from this dreaded habitation of man. The strange sounds roared in his ears, the strange smells overpowered his delicate nostrils, and he was so frightened that he did not know which way to jump.

The man kept his horse moving forward, still not letting himself relax. Getting his captive safely inside the yard would be the most ticklish task yet.

"Hi there, Jack! Open the big gate for me, I'll come in that way," he shouted.

Fury danced with alarm as more of the dreaded men appeared, and he lashed out with his hind-legs, warning them to keep their distance. There were harsh shouts and laughs from both the white and the black stockmen. Fury continued to dance angrily, lashing out with violent kicks which would have decapitated any man foolish enough to come within range, and by the time they reached the gate he was covered in a white lather of sweat. No matter where he looked, his enemies were there—jeering at him, laughing, and making jokes. He fought all the more as he was dragged into the yard.

The rider heeled his horse over to the far side as the gate clanged to. Then, after stretching his legs in the saddle first, he dismounted. Home!

Fury stood still in one spot. Then rage entered his heart, and

he started to buck his objection to everything. Gone was all
fear of the rope. He became a wild animal, fighting wildly for
his freedom. The man swore and moved his horse out of the
way, swiftly untying the rope and hitching it to a strong centre
post. Loud shouts greeted him as he walked his horse out of the
yard, while Fury continued bucking.

"What you got there, boss?"

"Starting to break 'em for the rodeo?"

"Ride 'im, cowboy!"

"Yippee!"

"Jest look at that horse buck!"

"All right, you men, break it up! I've not dragged him all
the way here to give you a free exhibition. I'm still boss here,
remember!" He spoke angrily, all the emotion of the last five
days coming to the surface.

There was a moment's silence; then the men moved away.

"Touchy, ain't he?" spat one.

As they went, so Fury stopped fighting and at last stood there,
exhausted and quite alone.

CHAPTER FIVE

The Breaking-in

D AN BAILEY was a third-generation Australian and a true bushman, in that he dearly loved his horses and understood them. His wife, Mary—a city girl who had given up the comforts and gay life of Sydney to follow the man she loved into the harsh bush life—shared his enthusiasm and understanding. They had a large number of well-trained stock-horses on their cattle station, and although they were not wealthy, they were happy and showed a small profit for their hard work.

With their neighbours from the next station, fifty miles away, they had combined in the drive to rid the bush-land of the brumby horses, not only to replenish themselves with more stock-horses, but also to preserve on the land the very valuable feed which was being carelessly eaten by the brumbies. During the hot weather, when they were waiting for rain, no man could allow precious herbage to be eaten by wild horses when his own stock was starving.

The land around Warrabell station was flat and monotonous, stretching far out towards the hills. The station house itself was raised on stumps, to let cool air circulate underneath and to dis-courage snakes. A good bore had been sunk deep into the earth, and water had been tapped and controlled for use in and around the house. It could be regulated easily by a handle, and they had six large galvanized water tanks placed at strategic points around the house, so that during the wet season the rain could run off the roof into the tanks and be saved. This water was then filtered and used for the house.

The outbuildings—like the house—were all constructed of wood, and they stood over plenty of ground. That was one thing that this country did have to spare. Space for every one and all! The precious commodity—that governed everybody's lives—was not land, but water.

The night horses were always kept saddled in one of the smaller yards, while the main bunch of horses was kept in one of the larger yards, where they had water—regulated in the dry weather from the bore—adequate feed, and space to wander.

The workers were as mixed as it is usual to find on outback stations: three good stockmen and a dozen aborigines. The former had their own quarters near the house, and the latter had their own bunk-house too. About three hundred yards to the rear was a small huddle of shacks and tents where lived the women and children who worked in the house.

The nearest town was forty miles away—not a long distance in the bush, but the station house was equipped with a pedal radio transmitting and receiving set for communication with the town.

Fury spent a very disturbed night. The strange sounds from the house upset him, and the fact that for the first time in his life he was closed in bewildered him. He no longer strained at the rope, but he kept throwing wild, anxious looks around him. On his feet all the night, he closed his eyes only for short periods, and with the dawn he was on the alert again.

There was so much happening around him. The cattle dogs —the kelpies—were barking outside the house, and the hands were at their early-morning jobs. Cows were being milked for the house, horses caught and saddled, the night horses fed and turned out. The various unaccustomed noises deafened his acute ears, and he was continually jumping. By now, though, he was used to the rope and had learnt to let it relax on his neck. He was feeling hungry. There was water in the yard, but it was food that he wanted.

When Dan came out he saw the animal watching him. He fetched a bucket of oats, climbed over the yard fence, and started to approach slowly. This was too much for Fury. He could tolerate men on the other side of the fence, but not coming near to him. He whipped round and fled to the extreme extent of the rope, where he stood trembling. Dan stopped still, placed the bucket on the ground, and slowly walked away.

Fury stared after him; then he turned his attention to this new enemy. The bucket stood there, grey and cold, and he snorted. What a terrible, strange world it was! There was so much that he could not understand. He advanced a few cautious paces, extended his nose, and sniffed at the bucket in sudden curiosity. As nothing happened he became bolder and moved nearer, every nerve alert, ready to spring aside if he was attacked.

Nearly half an hour passed before he had approached near enough to be able to examine the contents of the bucket. Then he imagined that he noticed something moving and leapt away in fright, nearly upsetting the bucket on to the ground. Back he came, though, and very, very gingerly lowered his head inside the bucket and looked at the oats. He snorted; the oats blew into his face, and away he leapt again. Then, as nothing further happened, he came back, put his head in the bucket, quickly lipped a few of the oats, and then stepped back. He lifted his head while he tasted the strange, dry, powdery pieces. It was a new taste, but how delicious! And he *was* hungry! He lowered his head and snatched another mouthful. He badly wanted to eat, but it was against his nature to lower his head and hide his eyes from the world while he ate. His eyes and nose were his guardians and sentinels, so, while he ate, he only put his nose in the bucket for long enough to take each fresh mouthful. He chewed the oats with relish, savouring the succulent flavour. How much nicer than grass! When the bucket was empty he licked it clean and promptly upset it on the earth with a clang. He made another frightened leap for safety, but the bucket just lay there.

So Fury learnt another lesson: that not all of what men bring is bad—that when one is hungry they can bring delicious, dry food, food which stirs the blood and warms the spirit, food which is really filling. But it was a long, long time before he was able to lower his head with complete trust into a bucket of feed.

There was a lot for him to learn, but he was an intelligent animal, and curious. He was ready to sniff at things and find out, and, if necessary, ready to fight them. Living his wild life had sharpened his wits and hardened his nature to a far higher degree than in a station-bred horse.

Fury was lucky that his new owner was a patient man, and Dan needed every ounce of patience to combat the suspicion of new things that Fury had inherited from his wild life and harsh experiences. Fury found that the man spent a lot of time with him, often watched by the stockmen in their spare moments.

As the owner of the station, Dan Bailey could do just as he pleased, but there were many ribald comments when he began to break Fury in. The average Australian stockman ropes the horse he wants to break, then by force clamps a saddle on his back and a bit in his mouth. Then he mounts the animal and rides to the finish. If the horse gets him off he wins, but the stockman is a superb rider, used to handling a horse in any wild country or wild weather, and very few men are thrown by their mounts. The horses are broken by this method, it is true, but the full trust between man and beast is not quite there. Trust comes after a time, but always with just that tiny bit of suspicion between rider and mount.

Dan Bailey, however, preferred the gentler and slower way of breaking a horse, especially when dealing with an animal of great spirit and pride. Fury was frankly puzzled by him. Dan would get hold of the rope, shorten it, and walk towards his horse, all the time talking slowly in a low drone. One day he touched Fury's neck, and Fury recoiled in horror and tried to pull away. Nothing was hurting him; it was just the alien touch and the presence of the man which frightened him.

The rope still dangled around his neck—it had never been removed—but he had the freedom of the yard and he did not eat enough oats to make him excessively high-spirited. Then one day a halter was draped around his face and neck. Dan talked to him and encouraged him with oats to distract his attention until he had put the halter on, and so Fury suffered the indignity without protest.

On another day he again experienced something new. Dan brought out an old saddle blanket. By now Fury did not mind the man's approach so much, as he had never been hurt, and there were generally plenty of the good oats to eat afterwards. But he eyed the saddle blanket doubtfully as Dan approached and then held it out for him to sniff. He strained back on the rope, eyes bulging, but, as usual, when nothing happened he pushed his head forward to sniff. There was a conglomeration of smells that seemed warm and friendly to him—smells of other horses. Dan started to swing the blanket slowly but persistently to and fro under Fury's nose. Fury shuddered and retreated, rearing his protest, but nothing happened to him. Gradually the swinging blanket came nearer, and suddenly, to his abject terror, it landed right across his back. He squirmed and danced to one side, and the blanket slid into the dust. Immediately he imagined all sorts of horrible things, and lashed out with his forelegs, as if it were a snake.

Dan picked the blanket up and started again, and so it went on for the whole of the afternoon, until at last Fury stood and submitted to the blanket being placed on his back. Dan led him forward, but the blanket fell off, and they were back where they started. Dan's patience, however, was inexhaustible, and by late evening Fury had accepted the blanket completely, allowing it to stay on his back while he was led around.

He was well rewarded with a good feed at the end of the lesson. Dan talked to him kindly and quietly as he fed and, before he left, deliberately threw the blanket on to the earth and left it there. Fury eyed the blanket suspiciously for a while, but by the next morning he was so used to it that he even walked over it.

The lessons progressed. Although Fury was not a free animal, he did not yearn for the bush. He had so many things to do and learn that his mind was kept fully occupied by everything. Now he was led around the yard with just the halter and the blanket on his back, turning to right and to left, stopping when the man stopped. During all this training he had known only kind, soft words from the man. He suffered no pain or fright, and gradually his latent hatred for the man was being replaced by trust and confidence—feelings that previously he had felt only for his mother.

There came the day when he had to learn about the bit. Dan slipped a strong head-collar over his head in place of the halter, encouraged him to open his mouth with a titbit, then slipped the bit into his mouth and buckled it up on the other side. He took great care in the fitting, and when he was satisfied he left the horse by himself, to think and ponder over this new and not very pleasant thing.

The bit itself was cold and hard. It did not hurt, but Fury was puzzled by the 'keys' that dangled from the bar of the bit, and he started to chew and slobber over them. Froth came out of his mouth—the first early sign of a good 'mouth' in a horse. The horse that has a dry mouth and does not slobber is usually the one that develops a hard mouth, or becomes a 'puller.'

When Dan came back he was pleased to see that there was a white line of foam around Fury's mouth. In the same spirit as Fury had learnt to accept the blanket so did he come to accept the bit.

The next big fuss was caused by the girth. Fury did not object when the breaking roller was placed across his back, but his belly flinched when he felt the girth being drawn up. But because he trusted the man he made no movement, standing quietly as Dan quickly fastened the girth and backed hastily away. Fury looked at him and then moved a pace towards him. Instantly he was aware of the girth—the tight feeling round his middle. The girth creaked, and that was just too much. He exploded.

He reared straight up high, leapt out in a huge fly-jump, and came down bucking. High, hard, fast, and furiously he bucked, but the girth stayed firmly in place. He could *not* move it, and at last he had to stop for breath. Dan came up and fussed him, but it was many days before he put up with the hard leather being strapped round his middle.

After the girth came the long reins. They were attached to the bit, run through the head-collar down through two loops on the roller and out on each side of his flanks, and ended up in very long reins, which Dan held as he walked behind—a good few paces behind!

At first Fury was made to walk straight ahead, guided by the man's voice and sometimes by a gentle flick of the reins when he was puzzled. Then he was walked in circles, turning to the right and to the left. They made an equal number of circuits on each side, so that his mouth would not become one-sided. The soft, easy feel of the man's hand was communicated by the reins to Fury's delicate mouth. In this way the mouth became sensitive enough to understand the slightest touch, and never at any time were its corners hardened or rubbed sore.

While Fury was learning these things the skin beneath and around his girth was slowly hardening to the feel of the leather, so that it was unlikely that he would ever develop girth galls.

All this training took much time and patience. It was not accomplished in a few hours or in a few days, but spread over a number of weeks, and the lessons were never long, so that he was never bored by them. Fury always knew that after the lessons there would be good food to eat and the quiet, smooth feeling of a brush sliding over his black, velvety skin, down his ticklish stifle to his hocks. He never attempted to kick. He had no reason to kick or fight, for everything was done with such quiet and slow thoroughness that he was never alarmed, and he associated only good, quiet things with Dan.

There came a day when some one else came with Dan, and for a time the old feeling of suspicion and distrust returned. But

Mary, like her husband, was a great horse lover and was quiet
in her ways, so Fury accepted her too. He knew that there was
a difference between her and his master. He noticed the different tone of Mary's voice, and that her scent was different. She
was smaller and quieter than Dan. She would come to him
with small things to eat—an apple or a carrot—generally
in the evenings when all was quiet and still, and they would
stand there quietly together, the great black horse and the small
slip of a woman. When she went Fury would raise his great,
finely-carved head and shrill out a whinny to her.

Some of the stockmen muttered among themselves at these
"goings-on" in breaking a horse, but Dan Bailey was a popular
if driving employer, and their pay packets were generous, so
they just dismissed the breaking shortly as a "crazy business."

At night Fury was let out and allowed to roam in one of the
home paddocks. These had strong, high wire fences, with
stout wooden posts every few feet, and there was absolutely no
chance of his escaping. Sometimes at night Fury would feel a
vague uneasiness and stand looking out over the bush-land
towards the hills, but the feeling was not yet strong enough to
make him do anything more than trot restlessly around the
paddock in aimless circles.

Early one morning Dan and Mary came out to him after he
had been fed. Dan carried a heavy saddle of the type favoured
by the Australian stockman, the high pommel and very high
cantle giving an almost bucket-shaped seat.

Mary fussed over Fury, rubbing his velvet nose and pulling
his ears affectionately. "You great, soft thing! I don't know,
here we call you Fury, but I think we should call you Softy!"
she teased.

"You'd better get back inside, Mary. I'm going to mount

him this morning, and he might have some objections!" said Dan with a grin.

Fury lifted his head and slobbered over Mary's hands; he watched her as she walked away. Then he looked at Dan and pushed out his nose for the morsel that he knew would be there. The bit was slipped into his mouth—not the heavy breaking bit but a light, working, D-ringed snaffle. Dan saw that the bit was in the correct place in the animal's mouth, not so high that it would pinch the corners nor so low that he could get his tongue over it. There was ample room behind the throat lash, and the bridle was a nice, comfortable fit. Then Dan lifted up the saddle for Fury to inspect. After some preliminary nose-blowing Fury gave a quick, approving sniff over the leather, and did not object when the saddle slid on to his back. The extra weight made him flinch for a minute, and he squirmed as the girth was drawn up and the stirrup irons dangled by his sides.

Dan carefully led Fury about a little to accustom him to the novelty of his tack, being especially sure to turn the horse in circles away from him, so that he could not possibly be kicked if Fury made any sudden movement. Then Dan halted, stood on his toes, and leant his weight against the saddle. Fury moved his legs to rebalance himself, but otherwise accepted all this strange behaviour quite calmly. Then Dan started to jump on his toes against Fury's side, but the horse did nothing, and, before he quite knew what had happened, Dan had vaulted on to his back, without touching the irons. Dan let his feet slither quietly into the irons, and he tightened his grip, waiting for an explosion. None came. Fury was too surprised to do anything. This new problem required thought. But he was not going to be allowed time to think about it. Dan wisely heeded the saying, "Beware of a thinking horse." Fury braced his forelegs and drew his hind-legs farther under him, to allow for the weight. Then he felt a gentle nudge in his ribs, and suddenly he was walking across the yard, with the man on his back. The extra and unfamiliar weight brought new muscles into play, and he had to get his balance afresh. The weight had to be allowed for at each step, and what with that, and the fact that he was being guided very gently with the reins, he was so occupied that he did not buck. He was walked quietly round the yard, stopping and starting, moving to right and left, for just an hour. By then he was very tired and puzzled with everything. He was only three years old, and he had learnt a good deal in the past few weeks.

Dan dismounted, removed the saddle, and made much of him. He brought him a feed and stood there talking to him while he ate. Then he quickly rubbed him down, talking all the time in the same smooth, quiet voice that he had used right from the beginning.

Gone was Fury's old enmity towards man. He felt a real desire to please this man. The man was master over him, but in such a kindly way that he never felt the urge to oppose him, as an animal with a fine spirit would oppose a bully. For the first time in his life Fury was entirely content.

Dan rode him every day after that, eventually going out into the open. To the great astonishment of the stockmen, Fury never once attempted to buck. He was well fed with oats, but as he was also worked well he never had the urge to get rid of excess spirits by bucking. He learnt many things. He learnt how to trot, and how to canter, changing legs on the diagonals. He felt the pulls of different muscles, and revelled in these new exercises.

One morning Dan took him out into the bush, on to a long, flat stretch of couch grass. He nudged Fury and eased his weight forward, and they started to move. Fury was not quite sure whether he was doing the right thing, as Dan had never extended his pace before. Dan nudged him again, and Fury started to gallop.

His paces grew longer, his large shoulders flowed under the black skin like rippling oil, his legs stretched out in great, swallowing strides. This was when his bent over-knees were such a help. They gave his stride just that little extra stretch, and the land under his hooves whistled past in a blur of browns and greens.

Dan leant forward, sitting lightly and quietly, balancing himself with his head, feeling as if some tremendous power had been let loose beneath him after months of being pent up. He let the horse run on. They galloped for one mile and then two, until Fury started to fight the bit. Then Dan spoke in his quiet voice, Fury's training responded for him, and he slowed down into a canter, and then into a trot. But his spirits were up, and he passaged sideways in excitement, although all the time he was in complete obedience to the bit. Finally Dan turned him, and he briskly trotted the three miles back to the homestead, arriving fresh and free of any evil intentions.

Fury knew that he had pleased his rider; he could feel by the swing of the man's body as well as by the tone of his voice that he had done right, and somehow it was very important nowadays to do right for this man. When Dan dismounted Fury stood there slobbering happily and rubbed his nose up and down the man's chest. That night he was more than generously fed.

After that day Fury was often galloped by Dan, and he

revelled in the speed which he could attain. He was a horse who really loved to gallop. He did not have a lazy nature, and his spirit was so high and fine that to extend himself with speed gave him as much excitement as bucking.

His muscles toughened up with all the work, and his legs became hard as the rock of his old hills. His carriage was more than that of a proud horse now—it was almost that of an arrogant stallion.

Mary came over to them both one evening while Fury was being rubbed down.

"You know, Mary," said Dan, "I believe this horse could race. That's something I've always wanted to do—own a race-horse. The money's in the stock, so we could afford to specu-late a little on racing. And if he was any good—why, just look at the money to be made out of stud fees!"

"Well, why don't you try him, Dan? There's nothing to lose, and often these wild-bred animals turn out the best," replied Mary.

"He's certainly too fast for a stock-horse," mused Dan. And he began to think seriously about the idea.

Throughout all this work and galloping Fury never once tried to buck. His trust in Dan was such that even when being shod he had stood quietly, never flinching or pulling back— because Dan stood with him, rubbing his nose and talking to him.

He had come a long way from the bush.

CHAPTER SIX

The Enemy

ONE morning Dan came out to feed Fury, but afterwards, instead of bringing the saddle, he went back into the house and finally drove off with Mary in the station wagon.

Fury spent the morning idly in the yard, wondering about the break in his usual morning exercise but not particularly worrying himself about it. There was plenty to look at in the yards.

At midday most of the men came in for lunch; only a few, including the three stockmen, were out either boundary riding or on other chores, The men ate their lunch and then sat in the shade of a tree and started to play 'Two-up.' Attracted by the noise, Fury hung over the fence, watching them and listening. The men became noisier and started to quarrel.

"You pay me now, fella, or there'll be much trouble," snarled the winner of the last game after the kip had been thrown.

The loser rose sullenly to his feet. He saw Fury; his eyes hardened, and a malicious smile broke out on his dark face.

"I've no money now until my next pay chit, but I bet my next two pay chits that I, Mangola, can ride the boss's black horse. I'll bet that against your winnings," he said.

There was a moment's silence, and they all looked at Fury. No one except Dan—not even Mary—had ever ridden him, but there had been much talk and discussion about the animal and about Dan's quiet and unorthodox method of breaking. None of them knew about the plans that Dan and Mary had conceived for the stallion. Although they knew that they would probably lose their jobs if they made the attempt themselves, there was not a man there who did not want to see the horse ridden, or did not fancy that he himself could ride the animal, in the bush way.

"Right, get a rope and catch him. I'll bring your saddle," said the first man. And so the damage was done.

Fury sensed the change in their mood and began to move uneasily away from the fence. One of the men slipped round and shut the gate of the far-side paddock, thus confining him within the small yard. Fury spun round when he heard the rope whistle through the air, but he stood quite still when it dropped over his neck, and did not fight it or the men as they approached. His training had been thorough. He felt a little apprehensive at the number of men that were around him, but as yet he was not alarmed. He did not flinch when the very heavy saddle was thrown on to his back, and he stood quietly while the bit was pushed roughly into his mouth. The men hung on each side of him, in case he tried to fight. Then Mangola jumped on to his back, and the rest of the men stepped back quickly and rushed to sit on top of the fence rails.

Fury stood quite still. He was rather surprised by it all, but he obediently awaited the signal to move off. The rider sat for a moment, waiting to see what Fury would do, his long legs gripping the saddle flaps, his feet encased, his huge, spiked bush spurs quite motionless. As Fury continued to stand quietly an evil glint came over the man's face; drawing back both legs, he raked Fury's flanks with the sharp, cruel spurs, flaying the skin off and leaving ugly streaks of red blood.

Dumbfounded by the shock, Fury stood quite still, trying to understand what was happening. The pain of the wounds was nothing compared to the sudden shock to his trust in man. The rider raked again, the spurs scoring down on the already bleeding flesh, and Fury exploded.

All the effects of Dan's patient teaching over those past few months seemed to be lost in a few seconds. Fury began to fight. He tried every trick that he knew to rid himself of the devil on his back. He hurled himself forward in spine-jolting, neck-snapping fly-jumps across the length of the yard. Then he whipped round suddenly and made across the yard again, with all four legs as stiff as props. But the man could ride. Every time the horse's hooves touched the ground the man's legs swung in an arc and raked Fury's wounded flanks, the long, sharp rowels biting deep and ripping strings of bleeding flesh. The blood spurted out and mingled with the dust, and the man was still in the saddle.

Then something snapped inside Fury. It was the same thing that had happened in the bush fire, and he reverted back through generations of high-spirited breeding to the primitive fighting animal.

He began to buck now, to buck in great earnest, to get rid of and to kill the thing on his back. He bucked as no man had ever seen a horse buck before. He reared up high and straight like a dancer, then came plunging down, nose between his forelegs, back humped like a post, legs drumming a deadly tattoo. He bucked so hard that it seemed he would throw himself to the ground. His movements were so violent and erratic that Mangola now had no time to use his spurs. Fury's head was whipping backward and forward, his spine was cracking with the strain, and there was a trickle of blood from the corner of his mouth. Suddenly the man knew that the animal he was riding was mad, and as suddenly as he knew it so Fury knew that he knew, and redoubled his efforts.

He heaved himself across the yard, sun-fished round—bucking, that is, with each shoulder low in turn—and came back again. Then he went round the inside of the fence, never once letting up the bucking. His coat was covered in a white lather of sweat and rage, his tail flailed the air, and his eyes were red and staring.

He changed his tactics and started to fly-jump out into space, bucking hard, very hard, on landing. Higher and higher his back rose, until he seemed almost to be suspended upside down, with power vibrating through every tiny muscle, and dynamite exploding in every movement.

Then Mangola felt his grip loosening. His head had whipped this way and that until he was dizzy, and he was shouting in pain. He had bitten his tongue, his thighs ached, and he knew he was going—going. He tried to clutch the flying mane, and then he felt himself hurtling through the air. He landed on the earth with a thud and rolled over to one side, his head still shaking.

It took Fury a few seconds to realize that he had shaken the man off. Then he saw him lying on the earth, moving feebly— the man who had hurt and tormented him, his enemy! He wheeled round and galloped straight at Mangola, his ears laid back and his mouth open, showing large, ugly, fighting teeth. He came to a halt and reared over the man like some grotesque dancer, waving his forelegs in the air, and then he came down and savagely pounded him into a lifeless heap of rags and blood and dust. Again and again he screamed his rage, and again and again he pounded until he knew that the thing, the enemy, was dead.

The onlookers, powerless to intervene, watched in horror. They had encouraged Mangola for the sake of the sport, not bargaining for his sudden display of cruelty. How ferociously his malice had been punished! Then Fury saw them too, and he charged straight at the high fence. He gathered his hocks under him, pushed, and sailed over the rails, scattering the men like a bunch of chickens. Once more a primeval killer, he spun round and chased them, and they fled, scrambling over the rails into the yard. One man was not quite quick enough, and Fury's swift bite stripped the flesh from his leg.

Then Fury turned and galloped off into the bush, the saddle tight on his back, the irons flapping against his sides. He blundered through a creek, scrambled up a rise, and instinctively turned to the only place where he knew he would be safe—his hills.

The bridle reins, trailing on the earth, caught on bushes and pulled his mouth, but he felt nothing. He galloped himself to a complete standstill, and stood shaking, hot, and bleeding, under one of his old gum-trees, near the base of the hills.

It was late afternoon now, and the sun was setting. Fury stood still, cooling down, and with the cooling of his blood his temper left him. The saddle was still firmly clamped to his back, and the girth had bitten deep into his flesh. There was a thick line of blood and hair under his chest and down his elbows. The long cuts from the spurs were coated with dust. His mouth was torn and cut, and he hung his head miserably. His body ached from his violent exertions, and one of his feet was sore. A shoe had worked loose, and was twisted into the

He came to a halt and reared over the man like some grotesque dancer

tender frog of the foot, so that it hurt even to move. He was not hungry, but he was thirsty. He had to drink.

He stumbled along the valley to a place where he knew there was water; on reaching it, he lowered his head and tried to suck. The bridle pulled at his mouth, and, in stretching his nose, he pulled tight the skin around his girth and felt the pain of the sores. He lifted his head and tried to shake the bridle off, but the throat lash was too tight. His sides were burning and throbbing, and he desperately wanted to lick his wounds, but that hurt, too. The tight girth cut into his skin whenever he turned his head. But he had to drink, so slowly, flinching at the pain, he lowered his head again and sucked up a mouthful of the water. He did not cry with the pain, as a human would have done. A horse is a stoical animal and suffers pain quietly.

It took Fury a long time to drink sufficient water. Then he felt hungry; but he was unable to move another step, so all that night he stood by the water-hole with lowered head, in abject misery. Gradually he stiffened up. The dust had settled firmly and worked its way into the cuts and sores. Pus was beginning to ooze out of his wounds, which swelled and throbbed, and his breaths came more frequently. His shins were sore, and his foot was so painful that he pointed forward with it. The saddle was still firmly on his back, and the flesh under the girth had started to swell. The bridle was still on his head. He half-heartedly hobbled a few paces towards a tree and tried to rub the bridle and saddle off, but he found that this caused him more pain, and he stopped.

Fury stood all the following day, alone and silent, with just the flies buzzing around the dried blood of his sores. In the evening he hobbled down to the water and drank again, and there followed another night of pain.

The next day a hard protective scab had formed on the cuts, a good protection against the flies, but a bad thing as far as nature was concerned, for now the poison could not get out, and started to seep into his bloodstream. He could do nothing. He just stood there.

Late that afternoon, although his senses were dulled with the pain, Fury received a warning of something approaching. A faint scent was wafted over the air; then it vanished again. He listened and heard the sound of a shod hoof, and his heart started to thud with fright and anger. As an animal will if it can, he tried to move away from the sound to safety, but he could not move far. His pain soon forced him to stand still, and he turned and faced the sound. His ears moved backward and forward, and his whole being was ready, if necessary, to fight.

The sounds approached nearer, and he saw two horses. The breeze changed slightly, and he scented the full impact of the man scent. His skin quivered, but his head came up high. Then the riders came into view.

Dan halted and dismounted, giving the reins to Mary, and he started to walk slowly towards Fury, speaking in his quietest voice. Fury's ears went right back against the sides of his head, and he was ready with his teeth.

Here was his enemy again. Man! Man who caused such blinding pain. Half of him was ready to fight, but the other half told him that there was something pleasantly familiar about *this* man. He snorted, and the man's smell came back to him. His memory pictured the man who had never hurt him by blow or deed, the man who had given him good things to eat. Perhaps this man would remove the torment from his back?

It took minutes for all this to go through Fury's mind, and all the time Dan approached nearer, talking patiently. At last he stood close to Fury and slowly offered his hand. Fury tensed himself ready to bite, and then he felt the new feeling again— the feeling of great calmness. He scented the man's fingers and then nickered a low greeting. He lowered his head against the man's chest and gave him his trust again.

Dan reached up and gently pulled the black ears, his eyes roaming over the many injuries. He stroked the muscular neck, automatically pushing the tangled mane back on to the correct side. Then he moved round to look at the long spur wounds, and his face darkened. He ran his hand down the legs, over the cannon bones; then he leant his weight against Fury's shoulder and lifted up the hoof. The shoe moved easily under his touch. He grunted, straightened up, and unfastened the girth, but the leather was stuck to the skin with dried blood and pus.

Dan turned and called to Mary, and she came with a bag and some water. She patted Fury's nose, and her eyes filled with tears. Then they started to bathe the girth with water, and after a while managed to prise it away from the skin. The saddle off, they removed the bridle. Dan did not bother to use a halter; he knew that Fury would not wander.

They both spent a long time dressing the wounds on Fury's flanks. They mixed an antiseptic solution, but Dan shook his head.

"I don't like the look of some of these scabs. There could be poison underneath. Did you bring a syringe with you?"

"Yes, there's one here with an anti-tetanus solution. Are you going to use it?" she asked.

"I think it might be a good thing. Here, you stand at his head."

Dan's quick fingers broke the sterile capsule, and he filled the syringe. Then he spoke to Fury, who was standing quite still but watching everything that was happening. Many strange things were being done to him, but he sensed that they were all for his good, so, even if some things were painful, he stood quietly.

Dan picked up a handful of loose flesh on Fury's neck, quickly slipped the needle into the skin, and pressed home the syringe. Then he withdrew the needle and dabbed the puncture with a solution.

"That should stop anything bad, but he's going to be lame for a while."

They camped out there in the bush, sleeping by the side of their fire, with just the cloudless sky overhead and the moon's rays as a sheet. Fury stood quiet and calm. He had been fed and watered, and the pain which he had felt for so many hours was going. The serum worked round his body, fighting the germs that had entered the cuts, and that, coupled with his youth and health, were already putting him on the road back to full recovery. The constitution of the wild horse is astonishingly robust.

The next morning Fury ate and drank well, and even started to move around a little for grass. It was a good sign. His ears were dry—they bore no trace of a sweat—and his coat was not dull or staring. But it was quite a long way back to the station, and it was still out of the question to ride Fury. Dan and Mary talked over the problem.

"The best thing to do, Mary, is to take him back in the cattle truck. I'll stay here with him. You go back and bring the men back with you—Kerry and Carter. You can ride back smartly—lead my horse, for I'll ride back in the truck with him."

"Right. Dan. I think that's about the best thing to do."

Mary had her breakfast and then saddled up the two horses. She mounted her own and took Dan's horse's reins in her right hand. A wave, and she was gone.

It was a long day. Fury heard the truck late in the afternoon. He pricked up his ears, raised his head, and ascertained the direction of the sound. It was still some distance away, but it was moving nearer. Dan noticed Fury's alertness and guessed what had caused it. Fury dilated his nostrils in suspicion at the sound. Previously he had only seen the truck at a distance, and as it slowly lumbered into view, bouncing over the uneven surface, his nostrils dilated a little more.

Dan strode over the ground as the truck grumbled to a halt, and Mary and Kerry, the foreman, jumped out.

"Glad you made it. All we've got to do now is to persuade His Highness to enter," said Dan with a grin. "Brought a halter?"

Mary tossed over a halter, and then went to help lower the back of the truck, to form a ramp. Dan took the halter and Fury, remembering, pushed his nose forward for it to be slipped on. Dan tightened the knot at the back of his jaw so that it would not slip and cut if he pulled back. Then Dan moved a step, and the horse followed. Fury was still a little lame, but his head had quite a jaunty carriage.

Fury did not like the truck, but Dan persuaded him to walk on, and the horse's faith in the man was so great that he followed him up the ramp, nervous and reluctant though he was. *This* man had never hurt him; this man he could trust—and trust is the most important binding link between man and animal.

Fury watched the truck and blew at it, and even paused and looked steadily at the ramp, but Dan did not hurry him. He let him examine it thoroughly, and then stepped on to it himself. The alert and intelligent animal saw this and, seeing that nothing happened to the man, allowed himself to be led forward. He placed one doubtful hoof on the wood, felt that it was firm, and quite quietly walked into the box, as if he had been doing it all his life.

The ramp was raised, closing the box in, the only light filtering through the wooden slats. Fury did not like to be hemmed in—it was completely against his nature as a wild animal—but Dan talked to him and ran his hand down his intelligent head, and the animal's doubts gradually disappeared.

The engine coughed into motion, and very joltingly they began their long journey back to the station. Inside the box Fury trembled at the first movements of the truck, but when he found that he was not being hurt he relaxed. He braced his four legs on the floor to balance himself against the jolts of the box, but even then he wobbled when they went down a deep creek. His head was pushed low against the man in the box with him. He nuzzled him trustingly, and Dan pulled at his ears with that quiet, affectionate movement that all horses love.

It was quite dark when they drew into the station yard, and when the ramp was lowered a wave of fresh air poured in. Dan turned Fury round and walked him down the ramp into the first large stable that was handy.

It was the first time in his life that Fury had ever been kept in a stable, but the cool, dark atmosphere was soothing. There were oats in the manger, hay on a rack, a bucket of water, and a good bed of straw. A horse could not possibly want anything more. Fury had undergone so many strange experiences with men lately that nothing really surprised him now.

He was already getting stronger. The scabs were still there, but lines of healthy, new, pink flesh were already appearing round the wounds. His hoof was closing, and the girth galls had hardened and dried. To all but those who knew and understood a bush-bred horse Fury's recovery would have seemed miraculous.

CHAPTER SEVEN

The Racehorse

FURY was in his yard the following week when the bush
police sergeant drove up to investigate the killing of
Mangola. Dan, Mary, and the sergeant walked over to
look at him.

"You can't blame a horse for going mad when he's ridden
by a madman. That horse is very high-spirited, and had never
been ill-treated in his life until that fool rode him," explained
Dan.

"You don't let Mrs Bailey ride him?" asked the sergeant
sharply.

Dan paused before replying. He was acute enough to see
what the question implied. If he said "No" that could be taken
to mean that he was afraid to let Mary ride him, but he could
not say "Yes" when she had never done so. He was not sure
how Fury would act with anyone but himself on his back—
especially now, after the killing. But he had to prove that his
horse was not a natural killer, or he might be compelled to
shoot him.

"She's never ridden him so far," he compromised.

"Well, how about now? If that animal's quiet enough to
carry your wife, then as far as I'm concerned he's no killer.
Don't think I'm being awkward, Mr Bailey, but I have my job
to do as well as you."

Dan threw a quick look at Mary and raised an eyebrow in
question.

She smiled back at him. "Of course I'll ride him. I haven't had any exercise to-day. Jack, fetch my saddle for me, please," she called.

Fury walked over to her when she entered the yard, expecting to find a titbit; he was not disappointed. Mary slipped the bridle over his head and popped the saddle on to his back. She wound some thick cotton wool round the girth so that it could not possibly pinch him where his sores were not hardened.

"Now, listen to me, you great, soft horse. For goodness' sake behave yourself with me," she whispered. Then, catching hold of the pommel, she was swung into the saddle, as Dan gave her a leg-up.

Fury stood quite still, awaiting the signal to move. He could feel the difference in the saddle, but most of all he noticed the comparative lightness of Mary. Her legs were not as long as Dan's, and her knees did not have the same strong grip. Fury was not alarmed, but just a little puzzled. He was not sure what he had to do yet, but he was quite willing to do what his rider wanted; she had always been kind to him, bringing him juicy things to eat and fussing over him. Mary nudged Fury's sides; he walked away and then broke into a springy trot. Mary leant forward in the saddle, riding by balance more than grip, the wind whipping colour into her cheeks and tumbling her hair over her shoulders.

Fury behaved himself like a horse well trained in *haute école*. He walked, trotted, and cantered with collected and extended paces. He backed, then passaged to right and left, changed legs at the trot and canter, jumped two small fences—one from the trot and one from the canter—and finally brought his performance to a climax with a brilliant gallop.

Mary had never ridden such a large horse before—certainly not one with such speed, and with such concentrated power communicating itself to her own body. As for Fury, the feather lightness on his back, the delicate touch of the woman's hands on his mouth, and the feeling of perfectly balanced riding made him give of his very best. He had finally learnt the joy of man and animal being moulded into one and performing as a team. He could gallop by himself, but when his skill was combined with that of his rider the two of them produced such a blend of motion and artistry that the sight was hypnotizing to bystanders.

When Mary did pull Fury up she was as loath to stop as he was, but he obeyed gracefully, without fighting the bit. His steps were gay and strong, but quite smooth, when he finished. His great black head bent at the poll, obeying the slightest gesture from the bit, his neck arched beautifully with triumph, and he held his tail out in pride and glory, waving like a flag. Finally he swung to a halt in front of his audience, and they greeted him with shouts of delight.

"That sure is some horse you have there, Mr Bailey. My, can he go! Wish I could buy him from you," said the sergeant, and Dan grinned as he shook his head.

"I'm proud of him myself; that's why I was so sore about the killing, and why I don't blame the horse." He slapped the glossy black neck and smiled up at his wife.

"He's a wonderful ride, Dan. You never told me he was like this," she accused.

"I wasn't sure myself," he replied, and they laughed together.

"Well, I won't bother you any more, Mr Bailey. I'm quite satisfied. Let me know if you ever decide to race that horse, he can carry my money any time," shouted the sergeant before he drove off.

"I was quite worried for a moment," said Dan after the sergeant had gone, "but trust Fury not to let us down. I really do think we could race him, Mary. Try him out in one of the bush town races and if he is any good send him down to Melbourne. What do you think?"

She nodded agreement.

"But don't you have to enter him soon for the big Melbourne races?"

"Yes, I'll do that next time we go into town. Nothing lost, and perhaps something gained."

Fury listened to the murmur of their voices, half knowing it was about himself, but not, of course, being able to understand it.

So it was finally decided to train him as a racehorse. This meant a different routine. He was kept in during the day, and had plenty of work, both Dan and Mary riding him. He spent hours bending and circling, and walking and trotting up slopes and hills. Twice a week he was given a short, hard gallop. Sometimes Fury would feel so fresh that the temptation to buck would come, but Dan was very wise. When he sensed these moods, instead of cutting his corn down, he increased the working period, and at the end of the morning Fury would come back at rest with himself.

Some afternoons Mary would ride him round the station, gently cantering along, looking at the fences and checking up on the stock. Now and then she would dismount by some water-hole and sit on the bank and bathe her feet, while Fury would stand patiently behind her, his head touching her shoulder. Between them grew up one of those strange but fascinating

friendships between animal and man. Even if Fury felt the urge
to buck when Mary was riding him, he never did. He knew that
she was not as safe in the saddle as Dan, and he somehow sensed
that it was a great privilege to carry her.

In the evenings and at night he had the run of the large
paddock, with a three-walled shed to shelter in when the
flies were too bad. There was a trough of water in the paddock,
and even if there was no grass, there was always some hay
thrown over for him.

At nights he used to have vague spasms of restlessness. He
would sometimes stand for hours down at the extreme end of
the paddock, head held high, gazing out into the night. His
nostrils dilated as he took in the various scents wafted over the
breeze, and his brain was alert as it dissected and analysed the
scents, telling him what was happening out there. He had every
comfort that an animal could possibly require, but there
was something missing, and it was in search of it that he
would stand in one spot, listening and listening through the
night.

He was a bush-born and bush-bred animal—a wild horse.
True, he had been broken and was being trained for a job, but
this was really only a very thin veneer, a false shell that could
easily be discarded. Underneath was the real animal—the wild
creature, strong, arrogant, fearless, and masterful. It was his
birthright to be out there, free and wandering the bush; it was
the law that he *should* be out there, with a band of mares,
feeding, sheltering, guarding, watching over them, and repro-
ducing his kind. *That* was what he had been made for—to be
the leader of a herd of mares, and to fight to keep and hold the
leadership. If he lost he would die; that was as nature had
ordered. Only the fit and strong were to live; the weak *must* die.

Here he was now, though—a tamed horse, worked and trained for a destiny with man, given orders by man, his will dominated by a creature smaller than himself—so small that one blow of a hoof could kill him—but a creature that had a superior brain.

He was treated well and with great kindness, but he lacked the one great thing that he craved—freedom! Freedom to roam the bush-land again, to wander just where he wished, to scramble up the slopes of the hills, to push his way through the trees, breathing the sweet, heady smell from the eucalyptus and gums, feeling the joy of water under his hooves as he wallowed in the water-hole early in the morning. Freedom to stand in the shade of a tree at midday and switch his tail at the flies and mosquitoes. Freedom to wander and climb at night and stare at the moon, when the silver light mottled the grass with silver and glimmered upon rocks and stones. He longed to be able to stand high on a hill and look down at the world beneath his feet, to listen to the mating call of a lonely dingo, to hear the weird jokes of the laughing kookaburra, and see the free, easy sweep of the eagle's wings as he flew effortlessly on the air currents hunting for prey.

Freedom!

The station had a mixed bunch of stock animals, both mares and geldings, but no stallion, because Dan had never thought really seriously about breeding. Very wisely, he had kept the mares away from Fury, sensing the turbulent emotions which raced through the horse at times. Sometimes on the night wind, though, Fury would catch the scent of the mares; he would trot restlessly around, then raise his head and scream out a greeting to them, and they would reply. The fences of the paddock were

high and strong, higher than the others. Once Fury felt such a
wild feeling that he cantered up to one, but he swerved at the
last moment, sensing that even he could not quite clear the
top rail.

His agitation began to show in his work. He was still obedi-
ent, but he would champ furiously at the bit, and in his movements there was a suggestion of pent-up dynamite. Dan sometimes felt that he was riding above a keg that was liable to blow
sky-high at any moment. One night he and Mary stood by the
yard and talked about it.

"I think we'd better give him a race as soon as possible. The
town meeting is next week, and though I hadn't reckoned to
run him so soon, I think it would be a good thing. He might
not win, but at least it will give him something else to think
about," said Dan.

"I've never known a horse quite like him, Dan. I wonder
what he thinks about when he just stands there and stares?"

"We'll never know, though I would guess it's about his life
before he came here. He's a real wild horse. By George, I wish
he could win a race! I'd make him into a stud . . . fence off part
of the land, and get a band of blood mares. The trouble is they
would only be able to have half-bred papers. We'll never find
out how he was bred," said Dan, his thoughts running on into
wild dreams.

"Who will you get to ride him in the race?" interrupted
Mary.

"That's the problem. I'm far too heavy. There's only one
chap. Remember little Jim Sharp? His father came out to help
us load the cattle last year. The boy's only fourteen, but sup-
posed to be quite a good horseman, and I understand he's going
to be apprenticed in Melbourne next year."

"But he's such a small fellow. Do you really think he could ride Fury?" objected Mary.

"Well, we can but see."

Jim Sharp came over the next day, riding a long-legged bay gelding, sitting like a small spot on the large horse. Mary liked Jim very much. His friendly nature and his mop of red hair and ginger freckles appealed to her. But she still felt rather doubtful whether such a small lad could control such a large and powerful animal. Jim, though, loved horses and had no fear of them. He offered his hand to Fury, and the stallion smelt him cautiously. He knew the boy was not afraid of him, and his smell was clean and good. It was also a kind smell. They brought out a saddle, and Jim mounted. He seemed very tiny, with his short leathers and jockey seat, but his hands were firm and gentle, keeping direct contact with Fury's mouth. Fury found that the boy was even lighter than Mary, though he knew that he sat differently. He could feel the weight in a different place on his back.

Dan would only let the boy trot and canter slowly to begin with, letting him get the feel of the animal's paces and power. Fury strode out obediently as he had been trained, head bent, paces collected. Finally Dan gave the signal, and Fury felt the nudge to increase his pace into a hand gallop. It was a pace where he did not really have to exert himself; his long legs flew over the ground, but he still kept much in reserve. He had a deep chest, which gave him plenty of room for his heart, and this chest had been developed to the maximum in his early bush life. He also loved to gallop. There was something so exhilarating in the movement that he always hated to stop.

Dan entered him for the second of the races, over a mile and a half. On the day of the race they took him into the town in the cattle truck, bouncing and jolting over the bush road until they got out on to the main highway.

The racecourse was packed with men and women who had come from cattle stations for miles around for this one day out. Cars and station wagons packed the car parks, and the crowd jostled noisily in the good-natured manner of folk who were having a day off work, and who had some money to spend. The bookies shouted and called their prices back and forth, and the general hubbub was loud, but not unpleasant—to the ear of man.

But to Fury the noise was alien and not a little frightening. He paraded in the paddock, head high and ears pricked nervously, wondering what it was all about. His black coat— which Dan had brushed to perfection—was already marred by a line of sweat starting high up on his neck and around his flanks. He danced sideways as Dan led him around, and now and then let fly with his legs in an experimental manner, making the people side-step quickly, and drawing attention to himself. The queer noises hurt his sensitive ears; the strange smells, and the smells of the other horses, excited him, and he humped his back and let fly a buck.

Dan shouted at him in anger; the last thing he wanted was a buck-jumping exhibition in the ring. Fury recognized Dan's new tone, and realized that he had done wrong. So he contented himself with dancing to right and left, keeping a clear passage for himself. Jim stood to one side, very small and white in the scarlet and black colours that Dan had registered. It was his first race, too, and he was as nervous as the horse, but he just had to stand still. Dan kept Fury walking, all the time talking to him, keeping his mind occupied, so that he would

not have time to get into any more mischief. Dan knew it was
fatal to let an excitable horse just stand and think.

The bell rang, and Jim mounted. Fury passaged to one side
and then stood still.

"Try and take it steady to start with, Jim, but he might take
some holding back," said Dan. "Anyhow, son, this is your first
race. Remember you're out there by yourself. I can't help you
now."

Dan squeezed the boy's arm, and off they went.

Fury cantered out on to the turf with hard, jolting steps. He
felt as if he was going to burst with excitement, and he did not
want to keep quiet. Although Jim was only a small lad, he
understood a horse; he leant forward, laid a hand on Fury's
thick neck, and spoke quietly to him. Fury put an ear back and
calmed down slightly.

They lined up at the barrier under starter's orders, Fury
standing rock-still, in amazement at everything. His heart was
thumping so much that the boy on his back could feel it
through his legs. The horses on either side were either standing
still or restlessly fidgeting, their jockeys sitting tensely forward,
waiting for the "Off."

Suddenly the barrier shot up, there was a shout, and the
horses were off—all except Fury. He stood still in sheer
astonishment. He felt the furious efforts of Jim's legs beating
his sides, and saw the other horses receding in a cloud of
dust. His mind was in a complete whirl, and he wanted
time to think. The roaring of the crowd was bothering him,
too.

But quite quickly he realized something. There were horses
in front of him, and leaving him standing there!

He reared up high in fresh excitement, leapt forward in a

huge fly-jump that nearly dislodged the boy, and came down running—hard! His head lowered and stretched out forward, his legs flashed under his body in fast but easy strokes, his tail spread out, whipping in the wind caused by his own speed, and his mane flapped on his neck. Jim leant forward and low, helping him all he could, driving with his legs, urging with his voice. And then there came to Fury the knowledge of what he had to do. Generations of breeding on his mother's side imparted to him the instinct and knowledge that no man could possibly have given him. He had to gallop fast and catch those horses!

Now he really did move. His legs worked like huge pistons, flashing out in black blurs, touching the ground and withdrawing too quickly for the eye to follow. His breathing was even and easy, and the pace was exhilarating to him. They drew up with, then past, the last horse and were in the central bunch of horses. Fury's eyes shone like black stars, and his nostrils were flared wide, showing the tiny red membranes as his lungs expanded to take in the extra oxygen necessary for such violent effort. One ear rose a fraction, as if contemplating the distance, then fell back flat again.

Jim sat there in ecstasy. His hands held the reins firmly, keeping the lightest of contacts with Fury's mouth, his knees gripped the saddle, and his body swayed to the horse's movements in perfect balance, timing, and co-ordination.

They began to pass the rest of the field, until there was one lone horse ahead. Another extra spurt, and they were alone out in front, with the winning-post looming up. For one second the thought came into Fury's mind that he had done what was wanted of him, and perhaps he should slow down, but he felt the insistent urge from his rider and kept up the pace. He loved to gallop, and the roars of the crowd, far from frightening him, now excited him.

They passed the winning-post in a burst of glory; but that meant nothing to Fury, and he kept on running. He was enjoying himself. As he galloped along he felt as if he was running away to the freedom that he had desired for the past few months.

Jim leant forward, rested his small hand on Fury's neck, and started to talk to him. Gradually the meaning of the words penetrated the horse's brain, and he realized what he had to do. His pace slowed down to a canter. He did not want to stop, but his training had been thorough, and he knew better than to fight the bit. Jim turned him round, and he trotted back into the winner's enclosure. Head high, ears pricked up, sweating freely on the neck but blowing no more than was necessary, he looked what he was—a very strong and fit horse.

The crowds packed the enclosure, but Fury did not take much notice, although he had never before seen so many people in one place. Dan and Mary fought their way into the enclosure and began to make a fuss of him, while Jim undid the girth and went to be weighed. Fury rubbed his head affectionately against Dan's chest and then raised his head. Some white froth blew and floated in the air. Fury knew that he had done well; he could sense Dan's pleasure. It communicated itself straight to him through the close companionship that he held with the man. By galloping he had pleased Dan and pleased himself.

As soon as they possibly could Dan, Mary, and Jim took the horse through the crowd back to the truck and drove off— three excited people and one contented horse.

Dan kept Fury in the stable that night. He examined his legs thoroughly, running his hand down the cannon bones and the tendons and looking at his feet. Fury had stopped sweating, had eaten a good mash, and seemed to have settled down remarkably well. Mary came up to him with some sugar.

"You'll ruin him!" said Dan. "He seems all right, but you can't really tell until the morning, when we run him out. Lameness won't show until he cools down—not that I expect to find any. There's no swelling of any kind."

"Wasn't he wonderful, Dan! Do you think he is fast enough for one of the Cup races?" she asked.

"Yes, I think he is. I had two offers to buy him to-day. No, don't be alarmed—I won't sell him. I was thinking about the Melbourne Cup. It's a tough race, with only the cream of the horse world, but I think this horse could give a good showing, and he might even get a place."

"I'm glad. Yes, I think we have a racehorse here, too. Didn't young Jimmy do well? Will you try and get him for the Cup race?"

"Too right he rode well. Yes, I'll go over and see his father. Come on, we'll leave Fury to his dreams to-night."

Fury had a few days' rest, with just some gentle walking exercise; then his training for the Cup started in earnest. Jim came over to ride him every morning before the heat was up, and Dan, mounted on a stock-horse, paced and timed the boy. The training included long, muscle-developing walks uphill, steady trotting for miles, and, twice a week, a hard, fast gallop. He was fed on oats three times a day and kept in the stable.

Some mornings Mary would come out of the house and stare at him in sheer admiration. Fury would be standing quite still, and he made a magnificent figure, fit for any sculptor to carve. His black, satin-smooth skin hung loosely over his frame.

His big muscles, especially around his legs, were relaxed. His great, clever head was high, his features finely wrought—his ears pointed, and his eyes looked straight ahead. His beautiful, arched neck rippled with muscular strength, and the hairs of his elegant black tail swung gently in the breeze. To the least expert of observers the powerful body of this magnificent animal told of speed and strength, and spelt out dignity and pride. He was what nature had made him, one of the finest creatures to be found on earth—a wild stallion.

Fury had reached his full growth now and was exactly seventeen hands. He had matured early, as some horses—and some men—do. He would grow no taller and would hardly thicken out any more, as already his body was as perfect physically as it could be.

One evening Fury was turned out into the yard while the Baileys had their evening meal, and it was then that he made a most interesting discovery. He had wandered down to the bottom of the paddock and was standing with his head over the gate, his tail idly switching at a few persistent flies. One bold fly hovered around his chest and bit him in a tender spot. He lowered his head to snatch at the fly, and, raising it again, caught the gate's latch. It lifted easily, and the gate swung open silently. One of Dan's idiosyncrasies was well-oiled gates. Fury stood for a moment and watched the gate open to its full extent before swinging back to close again; then he calmly walked out into the open. It took him a few seconds before he realized what had happened, and the glorious knowledge burst on him that he was FREE!

It was such a long time since he had been by himself, without a rider to tell him what to do, that he stood for a moment in indecision. Everything was quiet. There were just a few lights on in the house, and as yet hardly any animal sounds in the bush. He moved off with his long and carelessly easy walk, his head swinging as he listened and breathed the air—which, although the same air as in the paddock, seemed different to him now. Suddenly he began to trot. He carried his tail high in mock alarm, snorting with every step. He startled a wallaby and jumped, pretending to be afraid; then he broke into an exciting canter. It was wonderful to be free again—to be able to wander at will, without having to get permission from a rider. His ears flickered with the excitement as his feet started to speed over the grass.

Instinctively he knew where he was going before he had really decided. He had only one *real* home in the bush, and that was where he was returning. Back to his beloved hills!

All that night he moved steadily onward, not hurrying—for a horse will never hurry without urgent cause—but travelling at a sure, steady pace, until the first rosy fingers of the dawn found him a long way from the station, moving at an easy walk.

The sun crept almost reluctantly over the horizon, and its rays shot out into the sky, touching the clouds with coloured fingers—red, rose, purple, blue, orange, and yellow. It was one of those incomparable sights seen so seldom by man. The clouds changed their colours as the sun climbed higher. The trees were bathed in light rivulets of various greens, which trickled down the leaves as the rays filtered through their branches. The light carpet of dew glistened and shone in a million scintillating colours as the tiny drops caught the sun's rays, refracting them in little rainbows.

The animals and birds which had lain silent all the night now started to stir, as if the appearance of the sun had been a signal. A parakeet swooped on to a branch, poised there for a second, decided it did not like it, and then flew to another, its brilliant red and green feathers adding to the glorious symphony of early-morning colour. A bandicoot scuttled across the grass and disappeared; two wombats regarded each other, and then decided that it was too early to fight; a dingo rose, yawned, and stretched, before ambling off for food; a possum hid himself more thoroughly in the fronds of the tree. He was a night wanderer; now it was time for him to hide while others hunted.

A large kookaburra flew on to a branch and looked around him comically. He preened his feathers while he waited for an audience; then, satisfied that he had the world's attention, he opened his beak and started to scream with laughter. Not for nothing was he nicknamed the Laughing Jackass. A female kangaroo nibbled a succulent plant, holding it firmly with her small and tiny forepaws; then, startled at something, she dropped it and bounded away. A fly crawled out from behind a leaf and buzzed round in circles before disappearing straight up into the sky.

Fury stopped now and then to eat and drink. Then, as the sun began to climb higher, so did he. He sought out a piece of hilly ground, scrambled up the slope, paused, and looked down. He did not stay long, but cantered down and moved onward. At midday he had reached the valley and was walking along the animal and game trails. The familiar rocks and paths which he knew so very well were as if he had never left them. He cantered up slopes and scrambled on to rocky peaks like a goat, looked around, and then slithered down and explored somewhere else. A sweet crop of grass caught his eye, and he stopped and ate thoroughly, nipping the fronds with his strong white, cutting teeth, grinding slowly with his flat grinders, and savouring the succulent richness, which was a pleasant change after oats—no matter how nice they were. Then a drink. Even the water tasted sweeter.

Now that he was away from man his natural animal instincts were coming to the fore again, and most of all the basic one— the instinct of the stallion. There were no other horses around —that he knew. Either his ears or his nose would have told him of their presence.

That evening he fed in the valley. He wandered slowly around, picking the best grass, being choosy and fussy. Then he drank at a tiny, clean spring, making a lot of noise, blowing with his nose, and thoroughly enjoying himself.

He spent the night on top of the highest piece of land that he could find. He did not sleep as man sleeps. His eyes would close for a short period, while his ears and nose would stand sentinel. Then he would awaken, look around, and reassure himself, before going to sleep again. The instinctive caution of the wild animal, and everything he had ever learned during his wild life before he had been captured and tamed, came back to him.

He spent two days wandering through the valley and out the other side. He saw no rider, but that was understandable. The ground was extremely hard and dry—even an aborigine tracker would have found difficulty in following his tracks along the ground—and impossible where he had clambered about the rocks.

He knew where he was wandering. It was back down the way he had come after his last meeting with his sire. He did not hurry himself, although he did not stop or dawdle for anything that was not absolutely necessary to keep him alive. Food, water, and sleep were his only concerns. He was returning as a mature, strong animal over the track that he had travelled, seemingly so very long ago, as a raw and green colt. He was returning with the experience of man's training and with a body moulded to absolute fitness. He was returning as a stallion, coming back to claim his birthright.

CHAPTER EIGHT

The Chestnut Stallion

AT the end of that afternoon Fury was back at the muddy water-hole which had saved his life so long ago. It was still muddy, but there was more water there now than on his previous visit. As he approached his caution returned, and he tested the air thoroughly.

There was a slight evening land breeze coming up, blowing away from him, so that he could not pick up any scent. He moved over to the water and drank noisily, his ears back, listening. Then he raised his head, water dribbling from his lips. He had heard something.

A horse's nicker!

He raised his head high and blared an introduction and challenge. His chest trembled with emotion. There was a moment's silence, and then a harsh, brassy call answered. He moved out of the water towards the sound, switching his tail a little. Round the corner, hidden by the trees, were the two mares whom he had met, together with his sire, during the drought, long ago. Each now had a long-legged foal with her. Another horse stood at their head, but it was not Fury's sire.

Fury looked at the other stallion, taking in every detail, while the two mares nickered boldly to the stranger, and the foals trotted up to investigate personally.

The stallion was only a young animal—a leggy chestnut—and Fury knew instinctively what had happened. The chestnut, wandering perhaps from some far-off station, had found the two mares and had promptly challenged the old stallion for leadership. There had been a fight, and Fury's sire, old and weary, had at last gone down to the younger animal, who had in his turn taken charge of the mares.

The chestnut trotted springily towards Fury, blowing at the impertinence of this stranger in his domain, but Fury calmly ignored him. He gazed at the two mares and then at the foals. This was what he was meant for, to look after mares! Suddenly he felt free of the dreadful restlessness that had possessed him.

Then the chestnut reared, screamed, and demanded Fury's attention. He gave it. He rose on his hind-legs, screamed back, turned, and lashed out with them. The other horse was quick and evaded the action, rushing in with his teeth bared. They both half reared, forelegs flailing at each other's chests, and teeth snapping. Fury drew first blood, rending skin from the chestnut's shoulder. Then he flinched as his own skin parted. They swerved, wheeling and kicking, sparring for an opening, lunging first to this side and then to that, dancing and feinting, each trying to draw the other, each trying to get inside the other's defence of forelegs and teeth.

It went on for five whole minutes. Uttering harsh grunts and angry squeals, they fought with their two bodies locked together in fury. Then the chestnut began to tire. He had not the fitness of Fury nor the terrible driving purpose, and as soon as he started to weaken Fury knew. Fury pressed home his attack with more ferocity, snapping and tearing with his front teeth, striving for a fatal bite. Suddenly he was successful. His teeth drove through the chestnut's neck and met. They caught on the jugular vein, held for a moment, and then ripped backward. A shower of blood spurted over Fury's black coat. His teeth snapped together again and again as the chestnut began to sink. The chestnut knew he was dying, but his hatred gave him strength, and even on the ground he kicked and bit at his enemy. Then his heart stopped, and he lay still. A pool of blood formed under his throat, mingling with dust and soil. He was quite dead.

Excited, Fury reared and screamed his triumph to the world. Then he lowered his head and smelt the dead animal. Satisfied, he turned and trotted towards the mares, arrogant and proud. He was very pleased with himself.

The mares flinched nervously as he approached, cringing their skins as he cantered round them, shaking his head from side to side, waving his tail and making them bunch together. He was their master now, and they must and would know it. When he was satisfied that they did know it he placed himself in front and trotted away. The two mares and foals followed. It was not much of a herd—not enough to satisfy his instinct for long—but it satisfied him for the time being. He had a tiny harem to look after and protect.

Fury led them away from the muddy water-hole back into his own country, back to the place from which they had originally come. They spent two days travelling back to the hills, having to travel slowly because of the foals, but Fury revelled in his leadership. Slowly the memory of his months with Dan was receding, and in another few weeks his veneer of domestication would have vanished as he reverted completely to the wilds again.

Fury heard the riders at midday on the first day after getting back to the hills. As befitted a stallion, he spent most of his time now up high, where he could watch everything. As the two

riders approached he recognized them, and his feelings were
very mixed.

Dan and Mary were seeking him as they had done before, but
this time there was a difference. He had his own responsibilities
now, and there was a hard fight going on inside him. Half of
him wanted to run and take his two mares and foals to safety,
but the other half told him that no harm could possibly come
from these riders. As they moved nearer he came down from
his peak to the mares. They were alarmed at the close proxi-
mity of Dan and Mary. This was only natural, but Fury
wheeled on them suddenly, and they retreated from his anger
and stood quietly with their foals, while he proudly trotted out
to meet the arrivals.

They saw him coming and dismounted, leaving their animals
neck-reined to the earth. Dan walked forward to meet his
horse, and then, looking beyond him, saw the mares and foals.
His keen bushman's mind instantly guessed the whole story,
and he pushed his hat back on to the flat of his head and grinned.

"Well, I'll be darned. The old devil has gone and found himself a family. No wonder we could not find him! I wonder
where he picked them up?" He turned to Mary. "You know,
I wonder if these two mares are the ones that broke away with
the ugly stallion in the round-up. Do you remember?" he
asked.

"Of course. I'd forgotten all about that. It could be. Wait
a minute. Don't you remember saying you saw a black colt fall
during the drive-in and then tear off after the stallion which
escaped? Perhaps that was Fury, and perhaps he was eventually
driven out by the stallion and came back now and killed him,"
she said.

"Could be, could be!"

"What on earth are you going to do, Dan?" She began to laugh at the predicament.

"I'm darned if I know. He's hardly likely to welcome me on his back right now, but there's the race in two months' time, and I'm quite sure I'm not losing my stake money because of two mares!"

Fury watched them. Then Dan walked right up to him, held out his hand, and stepped back; Fury followed him. Dan gave him a piece of sugar as a reward. He picked it out of Dan's hand, chewed it gratefully, and then slobbered all over the hand, hunting for more. He felt the warmth and friendship being offered again and for a second relaxed his vigilance; he lowered his head against the man's chest and rubbed him in the funny little way he had.

"I trust you, but I am a stallion now. I too have something to do now. If you want me you must help me," he seemed to be saying.

He was very much aware of the power in the man and his voice, and there was so much attraction between them that when Dan stepped round to look at the mares and foals Fury did not object, but just stood and watched.

Mary came up and made much of him too. "Dan! He's certainly been in a fight. There's a long cut here. Not very old either, I don't think." She pointed to the wound that the chestnut stallion had made.

"We must get him back home. How?" Dan questioned himself. "I'm afraid we're going to have to put up with the mares; they're not the best, but they could be used as brood mares until I can get some better stock. We'll ride back and see if he will follow. If not, I'll ride him and drive the mares."

Dan and Mary mounted their horses, and Dan called to Fury

as they moved off. After some hesitation he followed them, but then he saw that the mares were not coming. Instantly he wheeled round, cantered behind, and drove them in front with nips and bites. How dare they defy him!

It seemed quite natural for him to follow the riders back to the station. After all, the station was another home to him—not a home like the hills, with peace and quiet and freedom, but a home with food and security.

But the mares did not like the station. As they neared the buildings they tried to run wide, but Fury was after them. His black body tensed with rage at this insubordination, and he ruthlessly drove them ahead with savage cuts and kicks. They poured through into the yard at a fast canter, the foals close to the sides of their dams in terror at all this dreadful strangeness, the mares equally frightened, but more frightened of their lord. The gate clanged to, and they were home.

"Well, what now?" asked Mary.

"Let them stay together in the yard to-night. I'll give Fury a feed and put some down for the mares. They might eat if they see him eat, and we'll decide what to do to-morrow," replied Dan.

Fury looked with pleasure at the large feed of oats. It had been nice to taste green grass again, but now it was just as nice to taste the oats. He tried to get the mares to copy him, but at the moment they were still too frightened of their surroundings. Later on, though, during the night, they sniffed and nosed at the feed trough, and after a few doubtful jumps they ate. So they too had taken the first step towards being broken.

In the early morning Dan came into the yard and with great patience, very quietly, and with unhurried movements began to make friends with the foals. They panicked at first, but Fury stood there stolidly, and after a while Dan was able to touch and fuss them. The mares were a little more difficult, but Fury, sensing what Dan was trying to do, helped by reinforcing the man's efforts with his own dynamic presence, and gradually the mares stood still and quiet.

It was not until the afternoon that Dan rode Fury out for his exercise. He had wondered what to do for the best, and had decided to ride Fury round the property, leaving the mares in the yard. Fury did not seem to mind leaving the mares. It was as if he knew that he would be coming back to them, and that until then they were being kept safely for him. His restless longing had been stilled for the time being. He had the company for which he had yearned, and he had work to do galloping. Dan was rather surprised to see how quickly he settled down again. Apart from being a little hot in his gallops and more keen on the bit, there was no change in him.

Fury loved the work-outs. The feeling of burning all that surplus energy in a way that he enjoyed thrilled him to the marrow, and he was always restless and keyed up until he had extended himself in a glorious gallop. He was given a great deal of work, but it never seemed to tire his frame, and he always came bouncing back into the yard, seemingly as full of vigour as when he went out.

The weather was becoming hot again. There had been no good rain for a long time. The colours around the house were changing with the dryness. The poinsettia tree, with its bright scarlet leaves, seemed unnaturally vivid against the white of the house walls and the black of the water tank. The leaves of the banana-trees in the kitchen garden hung limp and pale green. The flowers round the garden edge were dying off; only the jacaranda seemed to have a sweet freshness in its blooms.

The bark on the trunks of the gum-trees, paper barks, wattles, and eucalyptus was dry and brittle, and although the sap still ran deep inside the trunks, the roots now had to go a long way down for moisture. The grass was a pale brown, with just a tiny showing of insipid green here and there near the roots.

The cattle were on the extreme edge of the property, where there was some water. They milled around, trying to find enough feed among the coarse grass. The air at midday was too hot to do anything energetic, so man and beast rested. The horses stood listlessly, head to tail, switching the flies off each other. The birds stopped flying and fell silent, and even the mosquitoes seemed to disappear. The only creatures to show signs of life were the crickets; they never stopped their fiddling sound while it was daylight.

Movement became noticeable about four o'clock, when work had to be done, and when a light breeze usually came up. It was then that the horses were fed and watered, the cows milked, and the stock fed. But it did not really cool down until later on in the night, and Dan rose early in the morning, as soon as it was light, to work Fury before the heat began.

The two tiny foals suffered greatly from the flies; their skins were not as tough as those of the older horses, and the flies, knowing this, bit them unmercifully. The mares would stand there, switching their tails over the small bodies of the foals, but still the flies managed to bite. There was water in the paddock for the horses. It was in a long trough and came from the bore at the homestead. As the drought worsened Dan would come regularly into the paddock, look at the water, and then go back and look at the bore. Fury would come down to Dan, sensing something wrong, and nuzzle him, as if asking to share his comradeship still further.

The days passed, but still there was no sign of rain, and things were beginning to look serious on the station; the large galvanized water tanks were almost empty, and Dan had to ration the water strictly. The men all grew thick beards, and the garden was left to die. No water for shaving and none for the plants! The water from the bore still kept up a steady consistent flow, but Dan began to turn it off during the day. He knew that the bore was good, but he did not know how good, nor did he know how long the drought was going to last. If the bore dried up, then the whole station was doomed. He used to stand looking up at the sky, trying to gauge the mystery of the heavens, wondering when the rain would come. He listened to the weather reports every day, but the drought was widespread, and there was no news of any change. It had been a comparatively dry winter, and the tanks had never been fully replenished since the previous summer, and so they had no reserve to draw on. They had only the one bore.

Dan often talked to Mary about the water when they stood looking up into the sky at night.

"If only I could have afforded to have another bore—down at the end of the property. I'm sure there's water there. The rock formation is right. This wretched shortage of money. We could lose everything this year. Do you realize that?"

"I know, Dan, but it hasn't happened yet. I think it will rain," said Mary, and she murmured to herself, "but let it be in time."

With the dryness came the other great bush terror—fire! At the end of the property was a section of very heavily wooded land, full of tall trees growing tightly together. These trees thinned out gently as they came up the plain towards the homestead, but there were still a few which had been left to provide shade near the house. As with most Australian station homes, though, there was a large and broad fire-break around the house itself, an area where every tree had been carefully up-rooted and the grass cut short, as short as the blades of the mowing machine would cut. Inside this fire-break stood the house itself, the outbuildings for the men and the animals, and one small yard. The other yards were farther down among the trees and the longer brown dry grass.

With the dry, tindery feeling in the air Fury became uneasy, remembering the other time when he had been in a bush fire. Sometimes he thought he could smell burning on the evening air, and the smell nagged at his memory and worried him. Sometimes, too, early in the morning before the heat haze clouded the horizon, a faint pall of blue cloud could be seen hanging in the air a long way off. Dan, Mary, and the stockmen watched with serious faces, but the cloud never came nearer—and still it did not rain.

There was no wind yet to drive the fire in their direction, but they made preparations, just in case. Three night horses were now left saddled, and Fury, the mares, and the foals were driven into the small yard inside the fire-break. With water from the bore the stockmen filled every drum and barrel, placing them at various points for immediate use. They kept the station wagon filled with petrol and oil, in case they had to run for it.

Dan went over the fire-break one morning on the tractor, pulling the mowing machine and cutting the grass down so close that he blunted the blades. The men drove all the small stock, the few dairy cows that were kept, the pigs, the hens, and all the animals that were used for general purposes on the station, from the distant paddocks into those near the house.

On another morning Dan rode Fury out to the end of the
property, where they rounded up the beef cattle and drove
them away from the trees, nearer to the homestead.

It was the first time that Fury had been ridden as a true stock-
horse, and at first he was a little bewildered. Then he entered
into the fun of the job. He wheeled and chased after truculent
steers as if he had always been doing it, and although he was not
as nimble as some of the other horses, he put up quite a good
show. It was the first time, too, that he had been worked right
away from his mares, but this did not worry him. He had such
complete trust in Dan that he knew he would be taken back to
them, and that no harm would come to them.

They drove the bellowing steers on, and then let them
wander loose again. But there was little feed for them. Dan
debated in his mind whether to drive them up to the house or
to leave them where they were. Either action could be wrong.
If they stayed where they were they would be short of feed, and
still exposed to danger if the fire came. If they were driven back
nearer to the house there would soon be no feed left there, and
the fire might never come.

For a whole week nothing happened. They could do no
more to prepare against the fire; they just had to wait. Fury was
alert in the evenings now. He knew something was going to
happen.

Then one night Fury could sense that the time had come. As
the night went on so the moon rose, a brilliant silver goddess;
but it was an evil goddess, for with the moon's rising the wind
changed its direction. It began to blow gently, then with
increasing power, in the direction of the homestead.

It was such a gentle, subtle change at first that one could
hardly realize that the wind had begun to blow, but Fury knew

that the danger was at hand. His animal instinct was far keener than a man's senses, and he quickly turned and trotted round the huddled mares. He nosed them gently and again trotted anxiously around the paddock.

He could see for miles across the fire-break in the bright moonlight, and over the far-distant trees he saw that something had changed. The smoke cloud was moving in their direction. Fury could smell the fire, the hated bush fire, and he was afraid. The vivid picture came back to him of himself near death as a colt, and his heart began to thud painfully. In his panic he cantered about the paddock and then, seeing the mares, stopped and quietened down. He must not show them that he, their lord and master, was afraid. Suddenly he flung his head high and shrilled a loud, appealing whinny towards the house.

Again and again he shrilled. A light clicked on, and Dan's head appeared at a window. Fury nickered his fears, and Dan, alarmed at this most unusual noise, looked around, trying to find the cause. After a few minutes he came down the stairs half-dressed, with Mary at his side. They came over to Fury and rubbed his nose.

"Now, what's all the commotion about? What's upset you?" he asked, looking around. Then he stood still, and the wind delicately fanned his cheeks.

"Oh! Dan," said Mary, "the wind's changed. It's coming in this direction." She went white.

"Right. Mary, go rouse the men. Quick as you can. I'm going to ride down and see what things look like," shouted Dan, and he ran back to the house.

In no time Dan was back with saddle and bridle. He led Fury out of the yard, shutting the gate firmly after him, and then he leapt on to his broad back.

Fury felt his fear going as he sensed the man's confidence, and he obediently trotted away from the house, down towards the fire. It was still quite a long way off, and it took them thirty minutes' riding to come in sight of the blaze. All the way it was obvious that there was a fire. They met all kinds of animals coming in the opposite direction, fleeing from the blaze in terror. There were kangaroos, wallabies, rabbits, bandicoots, dingoes, even slow-moving possums—all trying to escape. Two snakes slithered along past them, making Fury rear in sudden anger. He nearly unseated Dan as he came plunging down, and the man had to fight to keep his seat.

As they approached the distant trees the moon was suddenly hidden, and Dan strained his eyes to see if it was a cloud or a pall of smoke ahead. But for the moment it was too dark to see. They were forced to slow down, as they had begun to blunder into things, but they pressed forward at a walking pace. The wind seemed to have increased in force, and suddenly they could smell the fire.

The smell of burnt wood made Fury afraid, and he stopped and shuddered a protest. Dan slapped his hand on his neck and spoke smartly to him, and Fury was comforted by the feel of the reassuring hand; the cheery tone told him that Dan was not afraid, and so he too lost his fear.

They walked up a long and gradual slope and when they breasted the top they saw the fire below them. It was moving quite slowly as yet, but it was quite clearly heading in the direction of the homestead. The grass was well alight, and, fanned by the wind, the fire was burning and moving along the ground, spitting and shooting out tongues of flame. Flames were already exploring up the trunks of some of the trees, but as yet the fire did not have the strength to climb the taller trees and run out along the branches, jumping from one tree to another, spreading in the air as well as on the ground.

But Dan could see that it was growing rapidly. His eyes took in the details, and his experienced bush mind calculated. He noted the clearness of the moon, the speed at which the clouds moved, and the density of the smoke pall. There was no sign of rain, and his cattle were right in the path of the fire. If the fire did not strengthen they would be safe until the morning, but if the wind rose they would have to be moved. It would be a well-nigh impossible task to move panic-stricken steers on a night as dark as this. They would most likely stampede and tear off blindly—perhaps right into the teeth of the fire. What was he to do?

Suddenly he decided. "Come on, Fury. Let's get out of this," he said. And, wheeling the horse round, he turned back towards the house.

As the moon showed through the clouds they broke from a brisk trot into a fast canter over the rough ground. Jumping logs and gullies, slithering on his haunches down steep slopes, Fury longed to let himself go, but until they reached flatter land it was impossible. He came to the long slope leading up to the house where he had galloped so often, and then Dan gave him the signal. He set his ears back and broke into a gallop. Driving up the hill with all his force and power, he was still going fast as they neared the homestead, but he skidded to a halt in the yard as the men poured round Dan, ready for his orders.

CHAPTER NINE

Fury and Mary

I DON'T like the look of it, Mary. It's coming right this way. Now, you men, get some sweepers ready and saddle up the horses. If the fire holds its course we shall have to bring the cattle nearer home. They're right in its path. We'd better try to get them moving now." He shouted some orders, and the men moved off.

"Now, Mary, listen to me carefully. I think this is going to be a bad fire, but if the wind holds off we'll be safe enough here. Put Fury in the stable, but leave him saddled. Drive the mares and foals into the barn and shut them in. If there's any trouble while I'm not here get on Fury and get out. Understand?" he asked her gently.

"Oh, Dan, what about the cattle?" she whispered.

He tried to reassure her with a grin, but it was rather a half-hearted grin, and then he led Fury into the stable.

Fury felt puzzled at being in the box with his saddle on, and he hung his head over the opened top door. He saw the mares and foals driven into the large barn with the iron roof. There they would be quite safe, and he relaxed. He saw the activity of the men, and a horse being ridden furiously out of the yard back towards the fire. Then an odd, eerie stillness settled on the buildings. Mary came over to him and stood with a hand rubbing his massive neck—not talking, but just standing there in silent communion.

Fury could smell the fire easily now, and he did not like it at all. The wind had slightly increased its force, and he could easily detect a number of distinct smells. There was the dry smell of burning grasses, and the sharp, clean odour from the burning trees. But with these were mixed the dreadful smell of soot and smoke—and, most frightening of all, the smell of burning animals—animals which had been too slow or too stupid to move from the path of the fire, and which had been asphyxiated while they hesitated.

With the wind, the fire itself became visible for the first time from the homestead. There was a red glow in the sky, and now and again a great, moving flame could be seen through the trees.

Fury breathed deeply, exhaled noisily, and switched his tail; he felt like lashing out at the door with his hooves. But he did not do so. He knew that that would startle Mary. His senses were fully alert—missing nothing, noting and searching all the time. He had lost the sound of the riders now, and he stood trying to pick up the sound of shoe on stone, or a man's voice.

The glow was distinctly bigger now, and the harsh smell of burning was clear even to Mary's nose. She slipped away from the box into the middle of the yard and gazed anxiously out in the direction in which the men had ridden. Then she came back to the stable again.

Fury heard the riders returning and nickered in impatience. Suddenly they came into view, galloping straight up the slope towards the house. Dan flung himself out of the saddle and ran over.

"Mary, listen. The fire's worse than I thought. The wind's getting stronger all the time, and we could not get anywhere near the cattle. It's going to take us all our time to save this place. I'm going to turn the bore on full blast, and we'll hose the walls and roof of the house and buildings. You're to stay here unless anything happens. Got that? You're not to move away from here under any circumstances." Then he was gone.

The men turned the bore on, and the precious water poured into the trough and started to overflow on to the ground. The men connected a long hose and sprayed the walls and roof of the house and all the outbuildings. Mary and Fury heard the water splashing over their heads. Then the stockmen overturned all the water butts and barrels that had been standing filled, sploshing the water over the grass, running a wet patch round the entire homestead.

Dan's head appeared at the stable door, his face covered with smoke smuts and his hair tangled.

"That should do here. Don't worry if the fire comes over the grass; it won't live—everywhere is too wet—and I don't think you'll have any trouble breathing here. We're going forward to try and start a back fire-break. It's the only way to stop this lot. You stay here," he shouted. Then he was gone.

Fury watched the men tumble into the station wagon and bounce off into the night and the smoke haze. The fire was very near now, and the noise was frightening. It roared, then hissed, then roared again, and one side of the sky was a deep crimson, where the glow of the flames was reflected on the clouds. The smoke cloud drifted overhead, carried by the wind, and the air was full of minute particles of soot and smuts and charred fragments of grass and wood, which floated down, settling on everything around.

Fury watched the fire running slowly up the slope towards the house, and he whinnied his nervousness. Mary, standing beside him inside the box, felt the same fear and anxiety.

The fire was like a huge, devouring monster. It moved steadily forward, never pausing, a brilliantly coloured carpet of red, yellow, and orange flame. It rushed up the large trees, danced fantastically among the branches, eating them bare, and then launched itself through the air to the branches of another tree. Some of the trees—especially the gums—exploded with loud bangs before they tumbled grotesquely and crashed to the ground. The tinder-dry leaves blazed furiously for a moment and then fell earthward as a shower of hot smuts and sparks. Drawn by the heat, the grass bent towards the fire as it approached; the flames licked among the dry fronds, and a pile of ashes was left on the earth.

Slowly up the rise towards the fire-break and the house came the fire. In some places where the grass and trees were particularly dry and thick the fire leapt out of the main body in liquid yellow streams. The slope below the house was a moving mass of flame, and it seemed impossible that anything could save the buildings.

Mary stood with Fury, watching over the rim of the door. The fire reached the break and crackled and hissed at the edge. Baulked, it seemed to rear up in anger, but there was nothing that it could burn. The grass was so short that in places it had died, and the slopping water from the bore, as well as that which the men had thrown from the barrels, had thoroughly soaked the ground. There was sharp hissing as the fire reached the wet grass, and thick smoke poured into the air, making breathing a little difficult, until the wind reached up and drew the smoke high, spiralling it away into the sky.

For no accountable reason the wind then changed direction. The fire swung to one side, found fresh dry food, and began to blaze with renewed vigour among the young trees and untouched grass. In five minutes it had spread right round the fire-break, and the house and outbuildings sat safely in a magic circle, bathed in a red glow.

Mary watched the fire turn with a sigh of relief. At least their homestead was safe, if nothing else. Fury watched her step out of the box and look around. The roofs were still damp from the hoses, and the bore was still pouring gallon after gallon of water on to the soil, until it seemed as if there was a quagmire around the troughs.

The mares and foals were kicking and shrieking in the barn, but they were quite safe there, and it was impossible for them to get out. All the domestic stock, although badly frightened, were unharmed, and as far as Mary could see there were no dangerous sparks lying anywhere which could burst into sudden flame later on.

In fact, all seemed very well, and she came back and leant her head against Fury in relief. Then suddenly a thought struck her, and she looked at the fire again. Although it had turned to one side, leaving the house and buildings in safety, it was now very dangerous for the men. They had gone to try to start another fire, which would burn the land bare. When the main body of the fire reached this scorched earth it would die out, finding nothing further to burn. It was a very dangerous way of stopping a bush fire, but sometimes it was the only way—when there was not sufficient water, or when the fire was particularly large and fierce. The back fire had seemed a good idea, but now the wind had changed, and the men might be caught between the two fires. There was so much noise and thick smoke that quite possibly they would not notice the change in the wind's direction, and even if they did, they could die through lack of air if they were in a confined place.

All this flashed through Mary's mind. She entered the box, hesitated a moment, and looked out again. What was the best thing to do? If she went riding out there, and the men were all right, might she not even get trapped herself?

Then she made up her mind. "Come on, Fury! We must find the men. You must really go this time."

She quickly tightened the girth, led the horse out, and struggled to reach the stirrup iron, but her legs were too short. She looked around in frustration, then led Fury to the side of the rails, climbed the rails, and fell over the saddle.

Fury danced a step and then stood still. Everything was so confusing and frightening—more so now that he was actually outside, with the fire nearer to him. He felt Mary land over the saddle and then wriggle upright, and he stood quite still, sensing her insecurity. He did not want to stand still, but did so, although his heart was thudding. His head was high as he breathed in the smutty air, and he began to tremble with emotion and excitement. He felt the light weight of his rider on his back, and the gentle pressure of her legs and hands, and he walked off.

He was glad to be out of the box. It was against his nature to be penned in, and he had the yearning now to throw everything to the wind and gallop and gallop away from the noise and smoke and terror around him. But his training and education had been sound. He obeyed the bit, collected himself, and, even if his steps were jerky and excited, remained controlled.

The smoke swirled round them as the wind lowered, and for a moment the whole house was blotted out from sight. Fury lowered his head and coughed, and Mary tried to shield her eyes from the smarting cloud that bit into her eyes and racked her lungs. She turned Fury, not knowing exactly where she was, and then remained still for a moment, trying to get her bearings. The wind helped by lifting the smoke for a moment, and the house walls looked as if they were in a thick fog, silhouetted against the red glow of the fire. Mary glanced behind, calculated where the buildings were, turned Fury parallel with the flank of the fire, and nudged him into a trot out over a patch of ground which had already been burnt, and which was covered by dead cinders.

He jibbed for a moment when he realized they were heading for the fire. The fire was too near for comfort, even though he could not see it because of the smoke. But he had as much trust in Mary as in Dan, and when she insisted he obeyed. He broke into a rapid trot, jumping the small patches of grass outside the fire-break and leaping the smouldering logs. Not for anyone would he allow his feet to touch the horrible live flames.

The smoke wafted lower, and he had to slow down his pace. It hung over their heads, making both animal and woman cough; it closed around them like a cloak, hiding almost everything from their view. Noise was all around them—strange, terrifying noise—the sounds of the fire eating up things in its path, trees burning and crackling, grass whispering and hissing. The earth was hot to the touch of Fury's hooves. Suddenly he stumbled over a hidden log and nearly crashed down. Mary lurched in the saddle, shooting forward on the animal's neck and nearly falling off. She spoke, and Fury stood while she wriggled back into the saddle again. Then quite suddenly they were out of the smoke and level with the front edge of the fire.

The flames were running gently over the grass carpet, flickering, roaring, and flickering again, but never stopping their advance. The wind fanned them onward all the time.

Mary urged Fury into a canter, and he set off over the uneven land as fast as he could go with safety, and without falling down altogether. He leapt to the command easily—glad to get away from the fire, and feeling the urgency of Mary's words. His feet moved swiftly and surely, jumping logs and small bushes; he jumped over anything that was in the way that could be jumped over. It was quicker than wasting time going round obstacles.

They were racing level with the fire now, moving down a stretch of unburnt grass, going faster and faster as the going improved. Mary leaned forward, peering ahead, trying to see the men. Oh, where were they all? She called, but the words were whipped uselessly from her mouth. She reined Fury back, stood in the stirrups, and "Coo-ee-ed!" frantically, but the call was drowned in the sea of noise behind her. She heeled Fury on, and he eagerly responded, his mettle rising; they galloped wildly now, flying over the grass, with the fire behind them. They went through a gap between some trees, and she saw a figure waving a sack.

"Dan, Dan!" she screamed, waving her hand and pushing Fury even faster.

Dan, his face quite black with soot and sweat, and his clothes sticking to him in the heat, looked up in amazement. "What the devil are you doing here? I thought I told you——" he shouted.

"Dan, the wind's moved round. The fire's coming at an angle. You'll be trapped in the back fire. You've got to get out of here quickly," she shouted.

Dan looked round. In front, moving down towards them, burned the fire which he and his men had started, and closing in rapidly from behind, and at an angle now, was the main

Mary leaned forward, peering ahead, trying to see the men

body of the bush fire. There was not much open ground left, and the smoke cloud was descending again, hiding everything from view. It was becoming difficult to breathe.

"Mary, get yourself out of here. No, don't ask questions now. Ride for your life! Jim, Bob—get the men. Hurry! Into the truck. There's not much time to spare. Come on, get a move on, will you?" Fear made his tongue rough.

The men staggered up, hot, dirty, and very tired. Mary watched them climb and fall into the truck. The engine coughed and then burst into life, and she turned Fury and let him go.

He had been standing anxiously, dancing from side to side, impatient to be off; now he leapt forward into a fast canter. He knew that this was the critical time. There was fire all around him. His eyes flashed in fright, his ears were laid flat back against the side of his head, and his nostrils were wide open; he wanted to get away from it all, and he nearly unseated Mary again as he fly-jumped in the air impatiently. Then he felt the tightness of the rein and heard her voice speak harshly, and he steadied himself.

The two fires were closing rapidly now. There were only a few yards left between them, and nearly all the breathable air was gone. Fury shot through the gap at a wild speed. But, feeling the tugging of the reins, he slowed down reluctantly, turned, and waited.

The truck bounced and jolted towards the gap. It could go no faster over the rough ground without smashing something. The men at the back fell over each other; those in the cab bounced up and down. A small tongue of flame flickered out threateningly and touched the truck's body. Mary felt fear catch at her throat. The petrol tank was full, and she knew well enough that petrol could easily explode in a hot atmosphere

Then Dan jammed the accelerator flat to the floor, and the truck roared between the flames towards them.

The flames hesitated, as if deprived of their prey, and then rushed together. Red, yellow, and orange flames shot upward. There was a loud bang as the two bodies of flame met and the fire was crowned. Then once more there was the noise of the fire burning fiercely, the blinding colours, the painful smoke and heat.

The truck ground to a halt, and every one watched in silence. Fury jigged uneasily from one foot to the other, switching his tail in excitement; then Mary turned him, and they cantered home by another track where the fire had already burnt itself out at the edge of the wet fire break. A pall of smoke hung low over the homestead, but nowhere were there any signs of a fresh outbreak of fire, and Mary dismounted wearily and leant against the saddle. Fury stretched and lowered his head, champing at the bit, his neck and mane covered in sweat, small pieces of twigs and charred wood fastened all over his body and tail. Mary put her arms round the horse's neck and began to cry with pent-up emotion. The lorry grumbled into the yard, and Dan jumped out and raced over to her. He took her in his arms and rubbed a hand on Fury's neck.

"There now, it's all over. The fire's burnt itself out; there's nothing left anywhere for it to burn. I don't know what would have happened, though, if you hadn't warned us. By Jove, what a horse you are, son! Best day's work I ever did when I caught you." He reached up and pulled Fury's ears affectionately.

Fury stood there quietly, though his sides were still heaving, and listened to the man's voice, feeling pleased with himself that once more he had pleased Dan.

He lowered his head and rumbled out a happy nicker.

CHAPTER TEN

Everything at Stake

THE rest of the night was a miserable affair. They could not leave the fire-break because places were still smouldering. Fury was put back into the yard, and Dan drove the mares and foals out to him. They were absolutely terrified, but gradually they calmed down when they were with the stallion.

The next morning they did not see the sun when it rose, for the smoke cloud still hung low over the sky. Dan was worried. He wanted to know what had happened to his cattle, but he was also worried about the water. The bore had been running for a long time, and tons of water must have been used.

In the mid-afternoon Fury was the first to feel the change in the weather, and he knew that there was rain about. The air had a different smell to it, and it was not long before the men noticed the change too. The day became dark and heavy, lightning darted across the sky, and it began to rain, a little at first but gradually increasing in volume until it was falling quite heavily. Finally the rain plummeted down so hard that Fury, who was in his stable, drew his head in from the door. The rain lashed against the wooden walls and beat a tattoo on the roof. The men rushed for shelter, and Dan dived inside the stable, his shirt wet and clinging.

"Steady there, Fury." He looked out through the door. "Why the devil couldn't it have rained sooner?" he grumbled.

It was quite a long storm, and thunder and lightning dominated the sky for the rest of the day. During that time, though, the fire was extinguished. The rain drove the smoke away, and gradually the surrounding bush was revealed once again. The whole pattern of the landscape had changed. The familiar landmarks of trees and bushes had either disappeared or were just charred relics now. But the air was easier to breathe, and the fire tension had lifted. When the rain eased slightly Dan ran out of the stable into the house, clattering up the wooden stairs. Fury watched him go and then hung his head out of the door again, watching the rain, savouring the sweetness. He allowed the drops to patter on his head until they ran down in a broad stream.

It did not stop raining until the evening, when it was too dark to do anything but feed the stock. Dan brought round a net of hay for Fury and drove the mares and foals into the barn again. Fury called to the mares, and they nickered backward and forward, but they were all quiet during the night, breathing in deeply the fresher air and clearing the last traces of the fire from their lungs. It was so clean and peaceful after the turmoil of the night before.

As the dawn came so the last of the clouds was blown away, and a pale sun pushed its way through and shone down on the charred land. Gradually the atmosphere began to warm up.

Fury watched Dan and Mary come out to him with their saddles. Dan led him out of the box, saddled him up, and then swung on to his back, while Mary mounted the stock-horse. Fury humped his back and pretended to buck, but Dan squeezed him with his legs, and he changed his mind.

They went through the gate and walked out of the fire-break into a sad and dismal waste land. The ground was black with charred grass, and in places the earth itself was burnt and still warm, even after the rain. The few trees that were still standing—without leaves or bark, gaunt and weird—poked their branches at the sky like black skeletons. In some places the ground was spongy after the rain, but most of the water had already soaked into the parched ground, to find its way through the upper strata into the natural reservoirs tapped by the artesian wells which fed the bore.

Fury walked quietly, somewhat interested in the mare that Mary was riding. He flung his head about and would have liked to have passaged over to her side, but he knew that this action would be instantly suppressed by his rider, so he broke into a sprightly jiggle to impress her.

He felt a certain tension in his rider, but could not understand it, and wondered why there was no conversation between his master and mistress. Generally they talked together the whole time when they were out riding. Quite often during the ride Dan reined him in, stood up in the saddle, and looked around, as if searching for something. Then they would go on again. They had passed out of sight of the homestead, continuing down the long slope, when Fury smelt something in the distance.

It was a very harsh, acrid smell, quite new to him, a smell that he did not like. He pricked up his ears, raised his head, and tried to locate it. Dan noticed his agitation and released the reins. Fury wandered on towards the smell, curiosity getting the better of him. They breasted the rise, and there, stretched out in front of them, they saw the sight which was the cause of the smell. Mary gave a cry of horror. Fury felt himself suddenly reined in.

Straight before them, lying in tangled heaps where the fire had caught them, were the remains of the Baileys' herd of beef cattle. The bodies were sprawled around in heaps, and some of the carcases, already bloated, were covered with big black flies.

Dan swung out of the saddle and let Fury's reins trail on the earth. "Stay here, Mary," he ordered.

Then, with long, swinging strides, he strode down the slope towards the bodies. They were charred and in some cases burnt through to the bones. As he approached, the flies rose in an angry, buzzing cloud and hovered furiously near his head. Dan worked out what had happened. It must have been when the wind changed direction; the herd had panicked and tried to get away from the fire, but in doing so had foolishly allowed itself to be encircled. There had been no escape. Those that had not been burnt had suffocated from lack of air.

Dan saw before him the ruin of many years of labour, gone in one terrible night. He spun round and stumbled back towards the horses.

"All of them, Dan?" asked Mary, a catch in her voice.

As he glumly nodded, she began to cry. Dan went up to her and gripped her hand fiercely, and Fury sensed the frustration and rage in the man's heart.

"Come on, let's get out of here," he said bitterly.

The horses wheeled and then broke into a fast canter, away from the slope, through some relics of trees, towards the dried-up river bed. The riders eased up there, dismounted, and sat on the bank. The two horses lowered their heads and started to pull at the grass they managed to find, slowly sidling towards one another.

Dan rolled two cigarettes and tossed one over to his wife.

"Here, smoke this." He gave her a light, leant back against a tree-stump, and drew on his cigarette, deep in thought.

"What can we do, Dan?" asked Mary.

"I don't know. I just don't know."

Fury ate on; then, as he started after a piece of grass that was still growing, his head wandered near to Mary. She rubbed his nose affectionately.

"We haven't the capital to restock, that's a sure fact," said Dan, "and I don't want to get another loan from the bank. Might not get one, even if I asked. It'll take a lot of money to replace that herd. If only there had been the money for a bore down this end of the property. Still, it's no good thinking about that now," he grumbled.

Dan went on thinking, his brain clearing after the initial shock. He watched Fury, whose strong white teeth were nipping the grass close to the earth. Then a light dawned.

"We could always win the Melbourne Cup," he said.

"Dan, don't be silly. This is no time for joking," reproved Mary.

"I'm not joking. Some one's got to win it, and why not us?"

"But only the best horses in the country run in that race. After all, Fury has only won a small, unimportant bush race," she protested.

"Not so unimportant. People wanted to buy him. Remember?"

"I think it's crazy," she said finally.

"Look, Mary, it's the only thing we can do. The purse of the first prize would put us right. The horse is entered, he's been in training, and he has a great turn of speed. You said so yourself. Just think—if he did win we could keep him as a stud."

Mary looked at Dan, wondering if he was really serious, but the hard look in his eye answered her, and they both turned and looked at Fury. He did not look like a stock-horse, and he did look like a racehorse, but the Melbourne Cup . . . !

Dan did some rapid mental calculations as he watched the horse. "It's only five weeks to Cup day, too," he announced. "What do you say, Mary? Are you game?" he challenged.

Mary shrugged her shoulders helplessly and then nodded, and they both grinned at each other.

"Fury, come here," commanded Dan.

Fury raised his head in question and then moved over and started to lip at the buttons on Dan's shirt, pretending to pull them off.

"Now, stop that. I've no money for new shirts right now! Our whole future is going to be staked on you, you handsome devil. If you win this race for me, then I'll buy you the best bunch of brood mares this side of the border." And he slapped Fury's neck, making him jump.

Fury felt the sudden change in Dan's and Mary's moods and knew that they were pleased once more. He stretched out his head and made a mock attempt to bite Dan's arm.

"Come on, Mary. Race you back," Dan challenged.

They mounted. Dan squeezed Fury with his legs, and Fury leapt forward. They raced back to the station, Fury leaving the struggling mare so far behind that she was still out of sight when he cantered into the station yard, excited and pleased.

CHAPTER ELEVEN

The Melbourne Cup

JIM SHARP came over to the station to stay until the race. He rode Fury all the time; no one else was allowed on the horse. Fury was moved away from the mares, but he did not have time to fret about them, for it was work, work, and work. He was walked for an hour in the early morning, before the sun had risen. Then he spent a short time trotting, to build up his muscles.

Three times a week he had a very fast gallop; one of these was over the same distance as the race. Dan and Jim carefully measured a stretch of the bush-land until they had a stretch of exactly the same length as the course. The surface was fairly flat, and after Fury had galloped over it a few times there was a well-defined track.

When Fury came back from his work Dan used to groom him. He was brushed with the dandy brush, then worked over hard with the body brush, and finally with the wisp, before he was polished off with a white cloth. By the time Dan had finished his coat was like black satin, and nowhere was there a smear of dust or scurf.

Fury liked the extra attention and even revelled in it. When he was being wisped Dan had to tie him up because he would swing round with his head and try to nip him every time the wisp landed. It was only in fun, but the nips had a sharp edge to them. Then, when he could not nip, he kicked out with one hind-leg each time he braced his muscles as the wisp struck him.

The heavy stock saddle was taken away, and he was ridden with a saddle of feather lightness. Jim rode him with his leathers short and high, and Fury had to adjust himself to the boy's lightness and forward balance, but he found he could gallop even faster now. Fury knew that Jim did not have as powerful a seat as a stockman, and he could feel that the lad rode mainly by balance. His touch with the reins was lighter and more delicate; but, nevertheless, there was still a firmness in it that had to be obeyed. It never entered Fury's head to buck. He was given far too much work for that mischievous idea to occur to him. Whenever he felt fresh, and joggled about restlessly on his toes, he was sent into a sharp, long trot up some slope; this took the fidgets out of him and at the same time helped to improve his breathing.

Dan himself fed him. In the morning there was a light but well-balanced feed of white oats, chop, and perhaps a few beans. Later, after he came back from his morning work, a net full of the best-quality seed hay was given to him. At midday he had a server full of oats, with carrots and chopped apples as titbits, and at night came his main meal: more oats, with seed chop mixed thoroughly, and on different nights during the week, a bran or linseed mash. Last thing at night another hay net was left for him to pick. There was always a bucket of fresh, clean water left in his box, and a bed of good wheat straw for him to lie on. In fact, he was no longer a bush horse, but a pampered racehorse.

Fury was a good feeder and never left even the tiniest bit of corn. In the morning, at the first sign of movement from the house or any of the outbuildings, he usually had his head out of the door, nickering.

One day the blacksmith came out and saw to his feet. He was

still wearing ordinary riding shoes, but the blacksmith removed these and put some light racing plates on for a gallop. Accustomed as he was to heavy shoes, the delicate lightness of the plates made him sidle and passage, but that morning he flew over the ground in his gallop. Then the smith removed the plates, put the ordinary shoes back on, and took the plates away to make another set especially for the race.

Ten days before the race Fury's training was eased up slightly to prevent him from becoming stale. His feeds had been varied as much as possible, and his work was now altered to make it more interesting.

One morning he stood in his box as the red and black sheet was stripped off him before the saddle was placed on his back. The light sheet lay over the box door as he stood staring out. His neck was firm and hard to the touch—a sure sign of a fit horse. His big muscles hung limp and loose, his legs were fine and beautifully taut down by the tendons, and his feet, when Dan lifted them, were clean and sweet-smelling. His back had shortened up a trifle as he had grown, and was hard over the loins, so that it was impossible to make him flinch by pressing. His quarters were well-rounded, hard, and extremely powerful. His hocks were long and smooth, without the slightest trace of curb or spavin—either bog or bone.

He carried his head high, and his tail well set out from his quarters, in the manner of a thoroughbred. His coat shone and glistened with health and fitness, like "an advertisement for boot polish," as Mary put it. His mane had been inclined to hang over the near side, but Dan had patiently plaited it until it now hung, correctly, over the off side. He was a magnificent sight as he stood looking out over the box door, breathing deeply.

"Hope you're as good as you look!" muttered Dan anxiously. He slapped the broad quarters and shouted, "Come over."

Fury hastily pranced over for the saddle to be girthed.

Two days before the race Fury had his last gallop. When he pulled up he was fighting the bit a little. Jim leant forward, talking to him and stroking his neck, and Fury relaxed and listened to the boy's fascinating voice. He felt keyed up and as taut as a cord, after the good food and excellent training.

He knew that something was in the air. He knew, too, that what with all the attention he had been receiving, and all the extra food and work, a great deal must depend on him. Something exciting was going to happen, but what he could not tell.

Dan had arranged to fly Fury down to Melbourne for the race. When the day came Fury was driven to the local airport in the cattle truck, wearing his red and black sheet with the large initial "B" emblazoned on it. He wore knee pads—that was something else new—and his tail had been bandaged in case he took it into his head to rub himself with it during the journey. His mane was plaited, and as he danced out of the truck he really looked a racehorse. All he had to do was to prove himself.

The gear was loaded first: brushes, feed, nets, blankets, extra saddle and girth, spare bridle—everything that they could possibly want.

Then the time came for Fury to board the aeroplane. The gangway had been cunningly strewn with straw, but this did not deceive Fury once he placed a hoof on it. It was slightly windy, and the straw was rustling. Fury viewed the aeroplane with great suspicion, throwing up his head and blowing. This was really something new! The precepts of his bush training came back to him. "Look! Be careful!" his instinct warned, and he hesitated—one foot on the gangway, three off.

Dan did not hurry him, but stood rubbing his neck, letting him look all around him—at the aeroplane and at the silent, waiting men. Then Fury moved another hoof on to the gangway and lowered his head uneasily. What was this thing? Would it hurt him? He tensed his muscles, ready to kick or to bite, but all the time Dan's voice was steadily droning on, and he had to give his attention to listen to it. The steady, pleasant tones reassured him, but his wild animal caution made him doubtful. He lowered his head and sniffed at the straw, knowing that there was something under it, but when Dan began to insist he moved forward—very dubiously. The gangway creaked with his weight, but nothing else happened. Then, quite suddenly, to his own immense surprise, he was up the gangway and in his stall in the aeroplane.

The stall was not very large, and when the regulation airlines collar had been fitted, the ramp dropped into place, and the bar lowered behind his hocks, Fury was in a very confined space. This was far safer than leaving him with plenty of room. It was quite impossible for him to fall down if the aeroplane hit an air-pocket, since the four walls supported him.

Jim and Mary squeezed past, the heavy engines burst into life, and the aeroplane started to vibrate. Fury felt alarmed and wanted to kick, but there just was not the room to kick. He felt frightened at being trapped, and showed the whites of his eyes, but Dan reached up, patted his head, and began to pull his ears. The old, familiar gesture quietened him, although his eyes darted everywhere, trying to puzzle out this strange experience.

The aeroplane taxied down the runway, swung round into the wind, and began to move forward, jolting slightly. Then it lifted itself inelegantly and was airborne.

After a while Fury settled down. He listened to the strange noise, but gradually came to the conclusion that it could not hurt him. He relaxed and began to pull at the hay net. The fact that Dan was there, and was not alarmed, helped to calm him. Like most animals, a horse can sense, and will often copy, the moods of the people around him.

It was rather a long flight down to Melbourne. They flew over New South Wales, crossed the Victoria border near the Murray River, and gradually descended, to make a perfect landing at Essendon Airport, Melbourne, Victoria.

Fury walked quite calmly down from the aeroplane into the waiting horse-box, as if he had been doing it all his life. It seemed as if he was quite resigned to the strange things that man insisted he must do. But inside himself he was feeling restless. He had not had his usual exercise, and he was getting tired now of being shut into boxes where he could not see. As they drove out to the racecourse he restlessly thumped the box with his feet.

Dan quickly found Fury's reserved stable and led the horse into it. It was a very large loose-box. Immediately he was free, Fury turned round and hung his head over the door.

What strange, exciting smells! There were numerous people walking around, leading other horses. There were horses of all colours, shapes, and sizes, it seemed, but they were all beautiful creatures, all thoroughbreds capable of great speed. There were mares among them, too, and Fury began to whinny and nicker, causing a commotion as he was answered by the mares.

Dan stood watching him a little anxiously and then turned

to Mary. "I'll stay here for a while until he settles down. You and Jim get along to the hotel and get some rest. You in particular, Jim," he ordered.

Mary and the boy left. Dan stayed with the horse all night. Not for anything would he leave his precious horse now, on the verge of such an important event. To the great astonishment of Fury he made himself a rough bed in the straw. The horse nosed him inquisitively when he settled in, but then left him in peace.

Fury and Dan were astir early in the morning and were soon joined by Mary and Jim. Fury was given a light feed, and then Dan threw a sheet over the horse before the exercise saddle was placed on him, and Jim took him out for some light exercise. Jim walked and trotted Fury along the track and then let him have a brief canter, to "blow his pipes." Fury was very excited; he danced and passaged and eventually came back in a lather. Dan viewed this with some concern.

As he was being dressed Fury began to kick out with his legs, until, in exasperation, Dan spoke sharply to him. Fury, sensing the change in the man's voice, turned his attention instead to the head-collar rope, which he began to chew frantically, as if he was starved.

Dan knew the signs. He knew the horse was excited, and thinking too much. "You old devil! Now keep still, will you!"

Jim appeared later, nervous and tense. He looked a very small, thin boy against the great horse, but his feeling of fright lessened after talking to Dan and fussing Fury.

The hands of the clock moved slowly but surely, and the noises of the crowd were loud and sharp. There was much activity in and about the boxes now. Trainers and lads assembled around their horses as they were moved out of their boxes, and now and then there was a squeal as two horses met and expressed mutual enmity.

Dan slipped the bridle on to Fury and led him out into the very large yard. Fury's head shot up as he looked around, trying to see everything at once, trying to take in all these exciting smells and sounds. Dan knew of Fury's feelings and wisely occupied his mind by leading him around the yard and out into the paddock, keeping him on the move all the time, preventing him from thinking and becoming more excited.

There were people all around the rails and people in the paddock. Fury had never seen so many people, and he did not like it. He humped his back and let fly with his hind-legs. The bookies were shouting and waving their hands. There was a long queue outside the tote. Noise, noise, and more noise—enough to disturb the most placid horse.

Dan walked his horse steadily round the ring, keeping a firm and short hold on the bridle. Jim came over. He looked smaller than ever in Dan's racing colours, and Dan wondered a little. It was a great responsibility for such a young boy. So much depended on this race. What if the lad was too young? What if he could not hold Fury? A thousand and one doubts shot into Dan's mind, but it was too late to do anything now.

The bell tinkled, and the jockeys moved closer to their horses. Dan halted Fury and tested the girth, making sure that the saddle cloth, with the lead weights, was on correctly.

Fury stood quite still, intently aware of everything. He champed at the bit and lowered his head, snatching in impatience. He wanted to be off, to do something, not to stand around there. He felt keyed up. His heart was pounding, causing little nervous ripples to show on his black chest. There was a faint line of sweat on his neck.

He felt Jim slip on to his back. He jiggled sideways, and then halted as the bit checked him. He felt Jim's small knees grip the saddle flaps, and the boy's weight settle firmly. He flung out a leg in a mighty kick and was promptly checked.

Dan reached up a hand and laid it on the boy's knee. "I'm not going to say much, Jim. You're riding this race, but we're with you all the way. You know how much depends on this for us. Try not to let him get too excited at the barrier and don't let him burn himself out at the beginning. Good luck!"

Fury felt a nudge in his sides and jerked off with agitated steps, champing his bit, his heart pounding. Jim collected and steadied him, laid a hand on his massive neck, and spoke quietly. Fury responded. They cantered down to the post, Fury stretching out his neck, filling his lungs, quickening the tone of his blood.

The horses lined up at the barrier—a colourful array of fine-quality horseflesh. Some stood quietly; others moved around in impatience. One even half-reared, trying to dislodge his jockey. The starter almost despaired of getting them into a straight line for the "Off."

Jim sat quietly, with a short, firm grip on the reins. He sat forward, watching the barrier, every nerve tensed and ready for the start. Fury's ears were pricked straight ahead, and when he allowed his eyes to wander around to left and right his attention was always drawn back by his rider. He moved a foot and placed it down again. He was as tense as a finely coiled spring. The weeks of work would show their effect within a few minutes. Fury had suddenly realized what this was all about. This was a race, and he remembered the last one. Knowing what was going to be expected of him, he was pleased, because he loved to gallop. He mouthed his bit and waited.

The starter saw he had them, gave the signal, and the barrier rose.

Jim touched Fury at the correct moment, and they leapt forward to a perfect start. Down the straight they thundered, Jim sitting forward, and his body moving rhythmically to time with the horse. He was no longer nervous now. This was the real thing.

Fury had flung himself into the gallop with his usual zest and enthusiasm, but he felt the touch on his mouth and knew that for some reason he must restrain himself. He did not know why, for he could easily have gone ahead.

So the horses raced down the straight, fighting for good positions, a brilliantly coloured spectacle. Fury was boxed in on three sides, but Jim did not let that worry him at this early stage of the race. The horses flew along, their hooves thundering mightily on the track, leaving behind them a trail of fine white dust.

Jim ventured a quick look behind him. There was just one horse a few paces away on their off-side quarters, but he was already falling back. The horses in front had altered their positions slightly. Four were now in front of Fury, and two on his off side, with the rails on his near side. He was well and truly boxed.

As they passed the half-way post, hurtling past at a great speed, Jim thought it was time that he did something. Fury was running easily, but it was time they moved up. Jim eased back on the reins and moved his legs. Fury responded, but only half-heartedly. He was puzzled. This was not what he had expected. Then Jim repeated the signal, and he obeyed. To get out of the box he had to drop back and move right round to the outside. In doing so he dropped far back from the other runners, and a murmur of interest rose from the crowd. They passed the three-quarters mark, and Jim leant forward. They were at the rear of the field now and could see the hooves of the other horses pounding down ahead of them.

"Come on, Fury! Now let's show them," Jim cried.

And they went!

That was what Fury had been waiting for! Back went his ears, out went his neck and head, and his long, bent-over legs began to beat their own distinctive, rumbling tattoo. His hooves barely seemed to touch the ground as they swept back and forth in a glorious rhythm of power. His tail streamed out horizontally like a proud banner, his great muscles worked cleanly and easily, and his nostrils expanded, to send extra oxygen into his lungs. Past one horse he went, and then past another! The crowd stood and roared. Never before had they seen a horse come out like this from a boxed position. If only he could hold the pace!

Fury was a wild-bred horse. He could hold the pace.

Jim urged with his legs, moving his body to help, one arm twitching with excitement. They must go faster yet. The winning-post was very near. Only a furlong to go.

Faster, faster!

Fury felt the kicks in his ribs and leapt into the air, increasing his pace until he was moving faster than he had ever galloped before. He could go no faster.

Jim sat, enthralled by the speed—a speed that even Dan had never known. He sat perfectly still now. The horse was giving everything he had, and he must not lose or disturb his balance in the saddle. One more horse to pass—a hundred yards to go. Faster, faster! Out of the corner of his eye Jim saw the incredulous look on the other jockey's face; then they floated to the front of the field. It was theirs! They were first! First! The winning-post rushed up and went past in a blur of red and white.

Jim knew they had won and sat easy for a second in triumph. Then he realized that he must stop the running machine under him. He knew Fury's dander would be up, and that to pull the reins would be futile, so he moved his hands against the sweating, lather-coated neck, talking, talking. Then he sat back and eased on the reins. Fury's mind registered again, and he began to slow down, a little reluctantly. He did not really want to stop, not now. The boy moved again, and slowly the great horse's pace altered, and he slowed down into a canter, turned, and moved back towards the winner's enclosure. Head bent, biting the bit, neck arched, flecks of foam flying in all directions, sweaty, and perhaps a little tired, he came, and still he carried with him a magnificent air of triumph, of something achieved, of a great glory.

As they rode into the enclosure the crowd roared and threatened to break the barriers. But the police moved up and linked hands. The excitement was so infectious that Fury began to dance and jiggle again. When he could go no farther he jerked to a halt. Jim swung out of the saddle, undid the girth, and went off to be weighed. His small face was scarlet with joy.

Dan and Mary fought their way through the crowd, and Dan grabbed his horse's head. He was beside himself with joy, and, man-like, did not know what to do. There was another great roar of applause as Jim returned, and Dan grasped the boy's shoulder in a fierce, emotional grip, making the lad wince.

"Jim, I can't say much now, but thanks," was all Dan could get out.

Fury stood there, wondering at all the noise and fuss as he felt a sheet being draped over him. Steam rose from his body in a cloud, and lather dropped to the grass. This was his most glorious hour, he knew—but it did not please him. There was something missing. He had done what he had been trained to do, and he had pleased the people who mattered to him. But in a sudden great rush of emotion he knew that this was not the life for him. He shrilled a blaring whinny out across the enclosure, a whinny that was meant for the bush. These smells, sights, and sounds were not for him. Not now. He found that he suddenly disliked them. Gone was the excitement and curiosity of a few days ago. Gone was the feeling of joy. He tried hard to gather a faint whiff of his beloved hills.

The crowd deepened as the Cup was presented and important racing men approached Dan. But he continually shook his head to their talk, and at last drew a reporter to his side.

"You can quote this from me. As owner of the winner of the Melbourne Cup I say this horse is not for sale at any price. I'll be taking him back to my station, and he will become a stud. I will offer so many nominations each year to good-class mares for breeding purposes, on the condition that any mares sent for service will be allowed to run with this horse in the bush. Nothing else!" he said, as he hugged his wife's shoulders.

The rest of the day was a confusion to Fury—a day in which

he had no further interest. He allowed himself to be taken from the course in a horse-box over to the aerodrome, where he entered the aeroplane. All the way back in the aeroplane he did not touch his net. He stood holding his head high, and if horses can daydream, then Fury did on that trip.

CHAPTER TWELVE

Son of the Wilds

IT was very late when they arrived back at the station. There had been much excitement at the bush town airfield, but Fury had stood quietly, disregarding it all. He was not interested in anything, and Dan drove back to the homestead as soon as he could politely break away from the well-meaning townspeople who had backed the horse.

That night Fury was turned into the large paddock with the two mares. They had neighed and squealed at each other in their pleasure at Fury's return, but, even so, Fury trotted round the paddock in an aimless manner for most of the night. He was still not settled.

He was kept in the paddock for the next two weeks, going out in the early morning for gentle exercise only. His feed was gradually reduced from the heavy oats to a lighter diet, until he was eating more grass than dry foods.

During this "roughing off" process there was a tremendous amount of activity on the station. Lorry-loads of timber appeared with strange men and were driven off into the bush, and other men were busy around the homestead repairing the fences.

One afternoon there was a sound Fury had not heard for many weeks. Slowly driving over the land came the new herd of prime beef stock to replace the herd that had disastrously died. Moving slowly, not pushed by the stockmen, they went down the slope towards the far pastures, where the men were erecting fences and driving a new bore. The sound of their muffled bellows carried back for a long time after they had disappeared in a cloud of dust.

Fury watched it all, his nostrils dilating as he absorbed the not unpleasant smell of the steers. There was much to watch, but while all this activity was going on he was still restless and unsettled.

The weather was warming up again, although at midday the sun had not yet reached the full power that it would have later on in the season. The grass which had been so badly burned had grown through the ash and soot twice as thick and firm, and already the only traces of the fire were the charred bark of the taller and thicker trees. There was sufficient water for the time of the year. There had been a few night showers, and the tanks at the house were full; one was overflowing down the waste pipe, so that the bore was not really needed.

One day Dan led Fury into his box and shut him in, closing the top door as well. This was so unusual that Fury was immediately alert. The two brood mares had been driven into the barn with their fast-growing foals. Fury started walking around the box, calling out to the mares, and getting excited whinnies in response. Then he heard more noises and stopped walking to listen the better. His heart lurched and he stood and screamed a challenge. But he knew what the noise meant.

Mares! New, different mares!

He roamed round the box, frustrated at this imprisonment, and lashed out furiously at the solid walls. Gradually, though, all the sounds disappeared, and stillness reigned over the homestead.

Fury was kept in the home paddock for another whole week. The only times that he went out were when Dan rode him.

Fury could feel Dan's light-heartedness now, and the infectious mood transmitted itself to him. But they never went far from the homestead on these rides, and one morning Fury dropped his head and started to buck a protest.

Dan swung his body backward, riding the buck, and, pulling at the reins, checked him sharply. Then he turned him round, and they galloped down the length of turf that had been used for the training for the race.

"Steady, old son. You won't have long to wait now. The fences are nearly finished, and you'll be able to roam as far as you like in one direction, right to the end of the property at the end of the hills. You'll soon be free."

Exactly one month after the race Fury was saddled up, and Dan led him into the yard. Mary was waiting, mounted on one of the stock-horses and leading another on her off side. They rode slowly out of the fire-break through the trees, which were showing a delicate shade of green after the recent showers and the warmer sun. They rode all that morning and most of the afternoon at a steady pace. The air was pleasant, not too hot or dusty, nor cold enough to make them wish to gallop.

It was good to breathe and be away from buildings, and Fury's spirits rose with every step they took away from the homestead. He danced along on his toes, head high, nostrils breathing the teasing, tantalizing smells of the bush. His ears flickered as he absorbed all the messages floating around on the air currents and deciphered them, knowing what bush animals were near and why. His feet itched to be away, and he was so restless that he started to shake and tremble. His steps were jerky, as those of an excited and fresh horse always are. His black tail flowed in ecstasy, and his mane whipped from side to side as he flung his head about this way and that. The feel of the grass, soft and springy, tickled his feet, and he just *had* to hump his back and let off one buck.

Fury saw with excitement that they were heading in the direction of the hills, and he began to fling his head up and down, pulling the reins in his rider's hands. Suddenly he was halted, and Dan slipped out of the saddle. Fury stood quite still, his heart throbbing.

Somewhere, somewhere there was—yes, somewhere there were horses! The air flirtatiously brought another scent, and Fury analysed it.

Mares!

Many mares!

He concentrated again, ears hard forward, nostrils wide, neck stiff and unbending as he tried to find their exact location. Where were they? To the right, to the left, or straight ahead? The wind was wafting these sweet, alluring scents to him so quickly that he had great difficulty in placing the direction. Then he got it.

Straight ahead!

Mary dismounted as Dan slipped the saddle away, leaving the two stock-horses—both geldings—neck-reined to the ground. Dan led Fury forward to the crest of a rise, and there down below were the mares. Browns, bays, chestnuts, and blacks. All thoroughbreds. All looking up in wonder at this huge stranger.

Dan slipped the bridle off and stepped quickly to one side. But Fury did nothing. He was taking his time, drinking it all in. A great and sudden realization had come to him. *This* was his destiny. Here in this bush he had been born and bred. Man had come, man had taken him. Man had made him work, made him bow to his will, made him gallop and race. He had done it.

He had done it willingly for this man, the one who had broken and trained him. He had pleased him, and now this man had given him back what he had longed for—given him back to the place of his birth, and given him, too, his birthright—his own mares to look after, to guard, to fight for, and to breed for foals.

Fury stood statue-like on the crest, legs thrust out hard against the slope of the ground, head firm and straight, eyes, ears, and nose working—the three vital sensory organs which from now on would be guardians of the mares and their foals. Then he turned his great intelligent head, nickered low to the man, rubbed his chest fondly, turned, trotted down the hill and broke into a fast canter. He advanced towards the mares like a great conqueror, a picture of strength and power. His legs moved in a motion so easy and effortless that it was hard to follow.

The mares stood uneasily as he approached, and then scattered, watching him. He raced through them, head swinging low, his speed increasing; then he turned on one hoof and whipped round the outside of them. Faster and faster he went, until he was racing round in a gallop, all the time closing the mares into a bunch.

One large bay mare turned to test his authority, and galloped away from the bunch. Fury wheeled in rage and tore after her, ears back, teeth bared. In a few strides he overtook her, slashed her with his heels, and, as she wheeled in sudden panic, drummed with both his hind-legs on her ribs. The mare braked, turned, and cantered back to the others.

Satisfied that he had shown them he was master, Fury trotted to their front and cantered away. The whole herd followed him meekly.

Dan and Mary watched them until they disappeared from sight, fading into the evening twilight, until only a few dust clouds hung to show where the herd had been. Then they mounted their horses, turned, and raced back to the homestead.

That evening Fury led the mares to the place where he had always returned after troubles and dangers—back to the hills which had always given him peace and calm, safety without fear. They spent the early hours of the night exploring, testing the water, and grazing. Sometimes they reared against one another in mock fights, behaving more like skittish colts than adult horses.

As the moon came out Fury did as any well-educated stallion would do. He trotted effortlessly up the highest slope he could find, up to a rock where in a past dimly remembered he had spent that lonely span of time looking and longing for other horses.

The mares gradually settled down for the night, content that they had a guardian.

Fury on his lofty peak first tested all the air currents most thoroughly, lifting his head up and down, swinging it from side to side until he was satisfied that no intruder lurked any-where about. Then he allowed himself to snatch some grass.

As the moon rose and threw a silver curtain over the gum-trees, the wattles, and paper barks; as the crickets stopped their fiddling, and the remaining mosquitoes took the air; as a lone dingo howled a serenade somewhere, a deep feeling of content-ment came to Fury. All the tension of the past months went. He was free! Free at last! Free and wild! Doing what he had been born to do.

Somewhere in the distance lightning flickered across the sky as a storm threatened from the heavens, but Fury took no notice. His eyes scanned the beloved bush-land and hills. Below him were his charges, his family; inside him was the knowledge that he had done his all for man, and his whole being radiated with confidence and well-being.

He stretched his head high into the air, drinking in this delightful freedom, and looked again over his mares. Then he shook himself hard, throwing off the last taints of man. He was truly himself at last, what he had been destined for from birth·

FURY, SON OF THE WILDS